DARLENE P. CAMPOS

Behind Mount Rushmore

To Amanda, I hope you enjoy this novel all over again ☺!

Darlene P. Campos

6-8-17

First published by Vital Narrative Press in 2017

First Edition

ISBN: 978-0-9983364-8-0

This book was professionally typeset on Reedsy.
Find out more at reedsy.com

Contents

Dedications

To my great grandfather, Jose Alcides Martinez Tobar (1903-1994), who would wake up in the middle of the night to write and drive my great grandmother, America Isidora Villamar Naranjo de Martinez (1920-1988), crazy every time he did so. Thank you for passing on your talents and determination. Thank you, great grandmother America, for always being his inspiration and making his written works possible.

To my mother, Tammy Yasmin Martinez, who has supported my writing journey since the day it began. Thank you for all the home-cooked meals, the prayers, the ridiculous jokes, and your nonsensical quirks which have appeared in every single story I have written. My love for you is so deep, there will never be a tool long enough to measure it.

To my boyfriend, David Noé Alcalá, who lets me write without any interruptions or distractions. Thank you for always boosting my mood, your hugs and kisses, and all the surprise "I Love You" text messages. I cannot wait until you are officially my husband. You make me feel emotions I did not know I had. I might be a writer, but I could have never written the love story you show me every single day. I love you, teddy bear.

To my good friend, Javier Andres Pritchard, who read the first (and terrible) drafts of *Behind Mount Rushmore*. I am so lucky to have had you as a reader during my early writing days. You always told me one day I would have a book published and now, here it is. Thank you for your suggestions, your encouragement, and your open ears whenever I need a friend to talk to.

To all the creative writing/English professors and classmates I had over the years – this book would not be possible without you. Special gratitude goes out to Jessica Paige Wilson, Anthea Ara Rafique, Bertram Allan Mullin, Carla Erizbett Arellano, Donna Dennis Muñoz, Guadalupe Garcia McCall, Bruce James Martin, Laurie Clements Lambeth, and Aaron Reynolds. Go Coogs! Picks Up, Miners!

To all of the wonderful English teachers I had in public school, but especially to Carol Thielemann, my second grade reading and writing teacher, Terri Cyphers, my sixth grade English teacher, Laurie Wilmoth, my seventh grade English teacher, and Carolyn Giannantonio, my ninth grade English teacher. I owe the strength of my writing skills to you. Thank you for being my foundation. A big shout out goes to Meadow Wood Elementary, Spring Forest Middle School, and Stratford High School!

To every literary journal that has published my work – thank you kindly for giving me the opportunity to share my words with your readers.

Last, but certainly not least, to Jennifer Snider-Batula. Thank you for your homemade cookies, the coupon booklets, and your wise insight on this adventure called life. You are the best co-worker and neighbor anyone could ever imagine. When Fred Rogers talked about good neighbors, he was talking about you.

The following stories were previously published in slightly different form:

"The Friend" was previously published by *The Gap Toothed Madness*

"The Dance" was previously published by *RiverBabble*

"The Funeral" was previously published by *Word Riot*

"The Cigarette" was previously published by *Alfie Dog Limited*

"The Burst" was previously published by *Connotation Press*

"The Crush" was previously published by *Forever! Onward*

"Lost Angeles" was previously published by *The Aletheia*

"The Fork" was the 2013 prose winner of *Glass Mountain*'s poetry and prose contest, previously published by *The Writing Disorder* and featured in *Plain China*'s Best Undergraduate Fiction Writing of 2013 anthology

"The Return" was previously published by *Bartleby Snopes*

"The Wedding" was previously published by *Red Fez*

"The Bullet" was previously published by *Elohi Gadugi* and was the winner of the 2013 Sylvan N. Karchmer Fiction Prize, awarded by the University of Houston

Special Thanks

Special thanks to Felipe Campos for cover illustration

Lakota To English Glossary

- *Ate* (ah-tay) – Father
- *Ciye* (she-yeh) – Older Brother, said by men only
- *Hankasi* (han-kah-she) – Female cousin, said by men only
- *Hoksila* (hokh-she-lah) – Boy
- *Ina* (e-nah) – Mother
- *Kola* (ko-lah) – Best male friend, said by men only
- *Kunsi* (koon-she) – Paternal Grandmother
- *Leksi* (lehk-she) – Uncle
- *Misun* (me-soon) – Younger Brother, said by men only
- *Sicesi* (sheet-eh-she) – Male cousin, said by women only
- *Takoja* (tah-ko-jawh) – Grandchild
- *Tiblo* (tee-blow) – Older Brother, said by women only
- *Thanksi* (tawnk-she) – Younger Sister, said by men only
- *Toksa* (toke-sha) – 'See you later' also used as a form of 'goodbye'
- *Tunkasila* (toon-kah-she-lah) – Grandfather
- *Tunwinla* (toon-ween-lah) – Aunt, father's side
- *Unci* (un-chi) – Maternal Grandmother

*Special gratitude goes to Sam High Crane's Lakota lessons on YouTube, LakotaDictionary.org, and the Lakota Language Project at Red Cloud Indian School

The Friend

*P*ine Ridge Reservation is a big rez. It's almost 3,500 square miles and it has badlands, prairies, hills, and a river – the perfect playground for a kid. But as big as Pine Ridge is, I never really made any friends.

In third grade, my teacher said I should be in the smart kid class so the principal put me there two weeks into the new school year. I didn't know anyone in the room. During recess, I tried playing with the kids from my old class, but they all called me "big brain" and said I thought I was too smart to play with them. After school, I ran to Principal Big Lake's office to ask if he could switch me back to my old class instead.

"Of course not," he said. "You're fine just where you are now."

"I don't know anyone in that class, Principal Big Lake. What if I'm not as smart as you think I am?"

"Don't be ridiculous," he said. He reached into his desk drawers and pulled out a folder with my name on it. Then he flipped the folder open and shoved it towards me.

"You had the highest test grades for math, social studies, science, and language arts," Principal Big Lake said. "Look at this essay you wrote last year – you got the highest score in the history of Wolf Creek Elementary! You'll be okay, kiddo. Make some friends in your new class."

"Good morning, Nimo the genius!" Ate said the next morning at breakfast. He wasn't working again because his temp job was up, so he stayed home looking up job advertisements in the newspaper. Ina graduated from Red Cloud High School and was a janitor at Shopping Cart, a superstore over in Sioux Plains, which was around 40 miles away. Ate worked odd jobs whenever he could. In the last couple of years, he had been a plumber, a handyman, a groundskeeper, a janitor, and my favorite, a holy Lakota man. 'Holy Lakota Man' meant he'd go up to tourists on the rez and tell them he had sacred powers which could only be shared if they paid him first. His powers were giving people Lakota names, teaching them what he called sacred Lakota phrases and one of his sacred phrases was "I am a giant fool," but he said it meant "I am a warrior." He also faked blessed them in the name of the Creator. It was all a load of bunk, but sometimes he made more money by doing that than he did from his other odd jobs. I know the Creator didn't like Ate scamming people, but then I thought the Creator would understand why Ate had to do it.

"I hate the smart kid class, there's no one to play with in there," I said.

"What about those kids who live behind us? Gorge and Locust Ten Bears, right?"

"George and Lorraine, Ate. They're not really my friends either, they only ask me questions about homework when they need help."

"Oh yeah," Ate said and chewed on his doughnut. "That's too bad."

"When I was your age, I didn't have a lot of friends either," Ina said as she stirred her coffee. "Kids didn't want to play with me since they thought your tunkasila would kick them off the rez if they screwed up." My tunkasila John David Red Cloud was the chief of Pine Ridge until he died in 1989. I didn't think my tunkasila was going to climb out of his grave and ban anyone who wouldn't play with me.

"C'mon, Nimo, time to go," Ina said after breakfast. "If we don't leave now, you'll be late for school."

"I'm ready," I said with a sigh. Ate gave me a goodbye hug and then I followed Ina outside to her beat up Ford Fiesta. Her car always smelled like the cleaning products she used at work – a combo of bleach, lemon, and oranges.

"I packed you a yummy peanut butter and jelly sandwich and vanilla yogurt for lunch," Ina said when she pulled up to Wolf Creek. "And you eat it, Nimo Thunderclap."

"But Ina, that yogurt tastes like rotten cream," I whined. And she knew it did. She even said it did whenever she ate it. But we got most of our groceries from the commod office and it didn't matter how bad the food was – we always ate it. We sometimes ate it with gagging noises, but we ate it.

When I got to Mrs. Silver Fox's class, there was a new kid in my seat with a Batman lunchbox in his hands. He had white skin but his eyes and hair were dark brown like mine.

"Who are you and why are you in my seat?"

"Mrs. Silver Fox told me I could sit wherever I wanted," he said with a weird accent. He sounded like he was eating something or he didn't have part of his tongue.

"Well this is my seat, move it," I said and shoved his arm. "See? That's my nametag right there. It says Nimo Thunderclap, so get your own seat."

"Hey, don't tell me what to do, you butt munch!"

"Who do you think you're calling butt munch, you funny talker!"

"Boys! That's enough!" Mrs. Silver Fox said. "Park it and shut it. Good morning class, we have a new friend in our class today. His name is John David Gutierrez. He just moved here from New York City. His mother, Miss Running Bear, is our new 7th grade science teacher. Stand up, John David, tell us about yourself."

John David stood up with his Batman lunchbox in his hands. He was sweating from his forehead.

"Uh, my mom teaches science and my dad owns a really good restaurant in New York City. I like Batman, reading books, and riding my bike." He sat back down quickly. Even though his accent was a complete nightmare, I was happy to hear he liked the same things I did.

John David always sat by himself during lunch. I usually ate in the bathroom so nobody would see the commodity food Ina packed for me. But one morning, we were all out of commods and I sat next to John David.

"Hi," I said.

"Hi Nimo," he said. "Where's your lunch?"

"I ate it," I lied. "It was so good, I ate it all in two minutes. By the way, my name is really Geronimo, but nobody calls me that, you can keep calling me Nimo."

"Geronimo?" he said with his strange accent. "That's not a Lakota name."

"Neither is John David Gutierrez," I said.

"It is too," John David said. "I'm named after the last chief of

4

Pine Ridge." So I told him Chief John David Red Cloud was my grandfather, since I didn't think he'd understand the word 'tunkasila.' He started talking to me in Lakota. His Lakota was perfect, but he spoke it with that terrible accent.

"Why do you talk like that?" I asked him.

"Like what?" he said.

"Like that," I said. "Sometimes when I eat hot food too fast, it burns my tongue and it makes me talk funny. Is that what happened to you?"

"No," he said. "My voice is just fine. There's something wrong with yours." I told him there was something wrong with his voice and he said there was something wrong with mine. We went back and forth, saying our voices were just fine until we got sick of it and quit talking altogether.

I went with my parents to the commod office like we always did every first Saturday of the month. We stood in line, sweating, and waiting for our food. Ate had his GED study book with him and he told me one day, we would get all of our groceries from the store because we wouldn't qualify for commods anymore. He told me that since I was really little. I always believed him.

As we walked to Ate's truck with our new commods, Miss Running Bear pulled up her car next to us. She recognized Ina from high school and they caught up with each other. At the end of their long conversation, Ina told her she and John David were invited to our trailer that night for dinner.

"We just got food for ourselves and you're gonna give it away to two people we don't even know? Are you also gonna tell her to move in with us?" Ate said to Ina during our drive home. We went over a big pothole, making me jump up and hit my head on the truck's ceiling.

"Ouch!"

"Sorry hoksila," Ate said. "Just be glad I ain't driving down Slim Buttes road."

"Jay Eagle, I ain't seen Yolanda since high school," Ina said. "She just moved back to the rez. It's the least I can do to welcome her home. She's very sweet, you'll like her a lot. I can't wait until she teaches Nimo everything she knows about science."

"She's a science teacher? Then tell her to eat some of her beakers for dinner instead of our food," Ate said and Ina pulled at his ponytail.

When we got home, Ina started cooking and I helped Ate tidy up the place. While I swept some dirt in the living room, I bumped into Nellie's picture on the wall. It fell off, but I caught it right before it hit the floor. It wasn't exactly a picture of her – it was an ultrasound photo. Ina miscarried her when I was five years old. I remember being excited to have a thanksi and then being devastated when I never met her.

"Look at her," Ate said, loud, so Ina could hear him. "She's jumping off the walls. Even she's mad at Ina for inviting people over when we don't have food to spare."

"Jay Eagle, if our daughter's jumping off the wall, it's to make you shut up."

"Sorry Ate, I didn't mean to bump into her," I said. He patted my shoulder and put the picture back on its hook.

"She would have been four today, Nimo," Ate told me. "Don't forget to tell her happy birthday."

An hour before Miss Running Bear and John David arrived, the lights in our trailer went out. Ate and Ina hadn't paid the bill again, but they thought we'd have light for the rest of the weekend. They lit some candles and spread them out all over the house. At six in the evening, our doorbell rang twice.

"Jay Eagle, please be on your best behavior," Ina said when he put his hand on the doorknob. "Let's try to make this a nice dinner, even without the lights." Ate swung the cracked door open. Miss Running Bear and John David stood on the porch, probably wondering why the lights were off.

"Welcome to the annual Thunderclap Candlelight Dinner!" Ate said and let them inside. They looked around our trailer for some time. I'm sure they noticed the torn up couch, our old TV on a chair instead of a TV stand, Ate's underwear hanging on a string by the window, and the black mold on the ceiling.

"Oh! Laundry on the window," Miss Running Bear said as she walked to the table, one we got from the Puentes, a missionary couple who helped us out from time to time. "I hung laundry on the window in New York City too, much faster than going to the laundromat and fighting for a dryer. A candlelight dinner sounds so romantic. John David, look, the Thunderclaps have a boy your age."

"Nimo," he said when he noticed me. "I won't be talking at all tonight since my voice is too weird for you to handle, if you don't mind."

"Look, I'm sorry for saying you talk funny," I said. "It's just, I've never heard anyone else have a voice like yours."

"I'm from Bensonhurst. It's in Brooklyn," he said. "Everyone in my old neighborhood talks like this."

"Even the mutes?" I asked and he laughed.

"Yeah, I guess they do," he said. "In their heads, maybe."

During dinner, John David and me sat on the couch in the living room, eating bland chicken nuggets. He told me about his old school, his old house, his Costa Rican dad, and how he was upset over his parents' divorce. As he talked to me, his accent was still strong, but it didn't bother me anymore.

"Hey Nimo," he said when we were done eating. "Do you wanna play a game?"

"Sure," I shrugged. "How about truth or dare?"

"No, last time I played that, I had to kiss my teacher," he said with a frown. Whenever my parents didn't pay the light bill, I got flashlights from the coat closet and made a laser show on the walls of my room. I thought John David would think it was a dumb idea, especially since he lived on the side of the rez where people lived in houses and bought all their groceries from the store. I figured he had way better toys than me and a flashlight would seem like some kind of bad joke. But he went to the coat closet, grabbed the flashlights, and asked me where my room was. I led him to it, hoping he wouldn't notice how empty it was. I opened the door for him. My sleeping bag was bunched up on the floor, next to my bent over bookcase and a pile of secondhand clothes I also got from the Puentes just before summer ended. In fact, if it wasn't for the Puentes, we wouldn't have had much of anything.

"You sleep in a sleeping bag?" he said. "That's awesome. It's like you're camping everyday. You're lucky."

"Oh, thanks, I guess," I said. We sat down on the floor and turned on the rest of the flashlights. First we spun them around, but our hands cramped up, so later on we made some shadow animals. Even when making animal sounds, John David's accent was thick. I thought it was hilarious. John David didn't mind all my laughing.

"Hey, you know what would be really cool? If we could make the Batman symbol on the wall," he said. He put his hands together, trying to do it, but he couldn't.

"That looks like a butt," I said.

"Then it's the Buttman symbol, duh," he said. We high fived each other.

During lunch the next Monday, I waited for John David at a table, but Scott Black Bear sat next to me. He was Mrs. Black Bear's son. She was the assistant principal at Wolf Creek. Scott could do and say whatever he wanted and his ina never punished him. His dad, Noe Black Bear, was a handyman like Ate. They were both out of work, but sometimes they did small jobs together. Mr. Black Bear was much nicer than Scott, but not too bright. Ate always said Mr. Black Bear was so stupid, he didn't know how to fart.

"Peanut and jelly sandwich again?" he said. "You never eat anything else. Maybe if your dad had a job, you could eat real food like I do."

"This sandwich is way better than what you're eating," I said, even though Scott had a double cheeseburger and French fries for lunch.

"My ina says your ate is too dumb to get his GED anyway. And what kind of dumb name is Geronimo? He wasn't even Lakota," Scott said. Finally, John David showed up at the table and he told Scott to move.

"You're not the boss of me," Scott said. "You're not even Lakota. What kind of last name is Gutierrez?"

"My dad is Costa Rican, you idiot," John David said. "And what kind of name is Scott? Isn't that a brand of toilet paper?"

"Hey! Shut up!" Scott said. John David started chanting "Scott Toilet Paper" and then everyone joined in, even the lunch ladies. They banged on the tables, getting louder and louder until Scott got up and said, "INA! HELP!"

Mrs. Black Bear gave John David and me after school detention for getting the whole cafeteria to tell Scott he was toilet paper. When we were free to go home, we rode our bikes to Big Bat's gas station and convenience store to get some cheap toilet paper. While we were there, we also got some hot dogs and chips.

"Are you boys up to something?" Mr. Graywolf, the owner, asked as he wiped down the table next to us. He was a little older than my parents and a big guy at over six feet tall and about 250 pounds. His wife, Mrs. Graywolf, who was almost as big as him, made all the hot dogs and she never made a bad one.

"Nothing's going on, Mr. Graywolf," I said.

"Ain't usual for two young boys to buy so much toilet paper."

"It's for school," John David said. "We need the tubes for a project."

"Tubes, huh?" he said and turned to Mrs. Graywolf. "Hear that, Rebecca? They ain't up to something, they're just doing a school project."

"Claudia's the same age as them and she don't have no school project," she said. "I'm watching you boys. Calling Scott Black Bear toilet paper in front of the whole cafeteria. Who would have thought two boys could be so funny?"

"Yes ma'am," I said. "Thanks for the good hot dogs." She winked back at me.

"Tell your parents we said hello," Mr. Graywolf said when we were done eating. "And John David, you tell your ina she can have a free hot dog and full tank of gas. It's our welcome gift to you two."

"How did you know we just moved here?" John David asked.

"Oh, hoksila," he said. "This is Pine Ridge. Your privacy days are over."

On Friday night, we headed to Scott's house. We dressed in our darkest clothes and made sure we turned off the lights on our bikes.

"I've never wrapped a house before," John David said.

"What?" I said. "Are there no houses in New York?"

"Not a lot," he answered. "Most people live in apartments. I lived in a house, but I don't think you could wrap it, it's probably too tall."

"Just do what I do," I said. "My ate showed me how to do it."

When we arrived at Scott's house, we covered the trees and shrubs in toilet paper. We heard a car coming, so we dived into a bush.

"Do you think they saw us?" John David asked.

"No way, it's too dark out here. Wait, I think I hear them coming back," I said. "I can see them through these leaves." The car turned around and drove slowly past the house. It turned around a second time and then it stopped.

"Check that out, Steve!" we heard a woman say. "I haven't seen a wrapped house in forever! They did a great job, that would be an A plus in my gradebook."

"Isn't that Mrs. Silver Fox?" John David whispered. I nodded. Mr. Silver Fox stepped out of the car, laughed at the top of his lungs, and said, "Look at that masterpiece! Those kids know how to wrap!"

"About time someone wrapped Mrs. Black Bear's house!" Mrs. Silver Fox said. "I'd do it myself if I didn't have so many after school conferences." Soon after, they got back in the car and they drove away.

"Whew, that was a close one," John David said as we emerged

11

from the bush. "I can't believe we almost got caught by own teacher. We still have a roll to go. If we're quick, we can use it on that tree over there." The front door of the house suddenly creaked open and we jumped back into the bush. It was Mr. Black Bear. I could tell because Ate once said his footsteps were louder than Ina's snoring.

"Leann!" Mr. Black Bear said. "I think we won some kind of toilet paper contest!" He went inside the house, shutting the door behind him. We tossed the last roll up in the tree and we hopped on our bikes right away before anyone else caught us.

"Aw man," John David said as we rode home. "We should've left him a peanut butter and jelly sandwich."

"I did, it's on his porch," I said with pants in between.

"Wait, won't he know we wrapped his house then?" he said.

"What's the worst he can do, John David? Wipe our butts to death?" I said. "I guess his ina might suspend us if she finds out, but that's fine with me. Who ever thought staying home from school could be a punishment?"

"Nimo, what time does Big Bat's close? I really want to get another hot dog."

"They're open for another hour, let's go," I said and turned right. John David followed after me. We rode past Sioux Nation, the rez grocery store, and we went up and down some hills just for the thrill. John David said he liked Pine Ridge so far. He told me New York had parks, but most of the city was only pavement. He liked the hills, the grass, and the curves Pine Ridge had. I did too, but playing on Pine Ridge was a lot better when John David came.

When we finally got to Big Bat's, we had two hot dogs each and split a brownie.

"You're lucky, Nimo," John David said and licked some fudge

icing from his fingers. "I never share my brownies with anyone."

The Diploma

Most of Pine Ridge is poor and a lot of people don't work, not because they're lazy, but because there's almost nowhere to work. There aren't a lot of stores, restaurants, or banks like other places, so people get by any way they can. Ate only went to 10th grade. Whenever he did find a job, it almost always asked for a high school diploma.

"Dammit Josie, you left bread crusts in the sink again," Ate said on the morning of his GED test. "I can't do the dishes when I see something soggy." He was washing the dishes with his GED study book balancing on the windowsill in front of him.

"They'll fall right into the disposal," Ina said. "You hate the weirdest things."

"You hate it when I don't wear my hair in a ponytail," he answered.

"I do hate it," Ina told him. "Remember the time when we was dating and it was windy outside and you kissed me? All your hair got in my face, I felt like I was making out with a girl."

"Yeah, I felt like I was making out with a girl too," Ate said over the running water. Ina sighed, but she still smiled. She handed me a brown bag with a peanut butter and jelly sandwich and a bottle of water. Ate's test would last almost the entire day. I had to go to John David's house until it was over.

"If Miss Running Bear offers you something to eat, you take it," she reminded me. "If I get a bad report about you, you won't be alive to see fourth grade, okay?"

"When have I ever been bad, Ina?" I whined. She looked at Ate and then they looked back at me.

"Well, let's see," Ina said. "How many hours did it take for Nimo to be born, Jay Eagle? Do you remember?"

"Do I remember? It was seventy five thousand hours. You screamed so loud, all my hair flew off. This is actually a wig, Nimo. Come and pull it off."

"It's not my fault I took so long to be born," I said.

"What about the time you shot out my truck's windshield with your BB gun?" Ate said. "And how about when you was four and you ripped Ina's skirt off at Big Bat's because you kept pulling on it even after she told you not to?"

"Okay, I'm sorry," I sighed. I waved goodbye to them and started the bike ride to John David's. He lived in Cheyenne Estates where everyone had a nice lawn and their cars weren't painted with two different colors. We didn't live too far away from each other, but whenever I went to his neighborhood, I felt out of place.

While I pedaled down the street, I passed Spotted Elk College on Spotted Elk Road. It opened up a few months back. The college was three stories high and took up most of the land. Ate applied there to be a handyman supervisor and the college liked him a lot, but the job required a high school diploma, even though Ate could already fix anything. The college said if Ate passed his GED test within the year, they'd hire him. They even gave him the study book for free. As I made a left towards Cheyenne Estates, Ray Firebird stumbled in my way.

"I don't have any change, Mr. Firebird," I said.

"Right," he said. "Your ate still ain't working?"

"Nope," I said.

"He can join me if he wants, I make around fifty bucks a day asking for money."

"I don't think so, Mr. Firebird," I said, shaking my head.

"Tell him to think about it. I'll teach him how to jump. Watch this," he said and jumped in front of a woman walking down the street. The woman panicked so much, she threw a $10 bill at him.

"See Nimo? Ain't nothing to it. All he's gotta do is jump good. No job application necessary and hours depends on him."

"I'll tell him," I said and biked away as fast as I could.

"What took you so long?" John David said when I got to his house. He was sitting on his porch, eating a roast beef sandwich.

"Ray Firebird jumped in front of my bike," I said and chained my bike around his front tree. I sat next to him and took a bite of my peanut butter and jelly sandwich.

"I hope my ate passes his test," I said. "I'm sick of eating peanut butter and jelly sandwiches all the time."

"Your ate is smart," John David said. "He can fix everything, he makes the best buffalo burgers, and he's the best liar I know."

"Yeah, he's pretty smart," I said. For once, I wanted to see Ate come home from a job that wasn't temporary.

A week after Ate took his test, I went with him to the government office to get our commodity food. We stood in line for an hour and when we got to the window, Angela Brown Eyes read through the list of food for us to choose from.

"Carrots or green beans, chicken or beef, apple or orange juice," she said with big yawns. "It don't make a difference which one you pick, it all tastes like horse manure."

"Really Angela?" Ate said. "I've been coming here for years and you don't know what I want?"

"Sorry Jay Eagle, standard procedure," she shrugged and finished filing her nails.

"I'm getting real sick of coming to this place, son," he whispered to me as we walked to his truck with our new food. "You'll see Nimo, one day, we're gonna go to Sioux Nation and buy a hundred bucks worth of food. Then we're gonna come home, cook everything, and eat it all in one hit."

"That's gonna make us throw up, Ate."

"It might, son," he said. "But hell, it'd be worth it."

During the drive back to the trailer, Ate told me about a game he used to play with Leksi Gray Mountain. He said sometimes they'd go two or three days without food and they would compare how loud their stomach growls were. Whoever's stomach was the loudest got to eat first when food was finally around.

"I always won," Ate said and turned onto Sitting Bull Drive. "Always."

"Did you ever eat peanut butter and jelly sandwiches?"

"Breakfast, lunch, and dinner," he said. "Almost every damn day."

When we got home, we saw Leksi's truck parked on our lawn. He was visiting with my tunwinla Rosa and my two year old hankasi Lucille, who was also called Lucy for short. Leksi Gray Mountain graduated from the University of South Dakota at Sioux Plains in 1989 and he was a surgeon and a general doctor at the Sioux Plains Medical Center. Tunwinla Rosa got her degree in Psychology from Black Hills State in 1990 and she had her own office at the same medical center where Leksi worked. They had a nice house, nice furniture, and pretty much a nice everything, even a nice coffee maker. I looked at Lucille who was exploring the whole living room. Our old couch with stains and rips amazed her the most. She never saw anything like it before. Leksi Gray Mountain was much taller than Ate and his body looked healthy with all of his muscles. Tunwinla Rosa was around Ina's height and a little bit thinner, but her hair was always shiny and her face was always covered in makeup. Ina didn't wear much makeup except for some lipstick. She said she would sweat too much at work, so she didn't see the point of makeup anyway.

"When do you get your test results, misun?" Leksi asked Ate.

"End of the month or so," Ate said. "If I failed, I'll study until my eyeballs pop out."

"Don't do that, Jay Eagle, then you won't be able see how pretty I am," Ina said from the kitchen. She and Tunwinla were cooking chili with pieces of commod ground beef, the kind that looked like it wasn't ground beef.

"You still don't know if he passed or not?" John David said one Friday afternoon as we rode our bikes back home from Wolf Creek School.

"No, he hasn't really talked about it either," I said. "I'll ask him about it tonight." We waved to each other since we had to ride in opposite directions for the last mile. When I got home,

Ate was on the porch, carving a few spears to sell to tourists at Big Bat's. Ina wasn't back from work yet. I asked Ate if he wanted me to make her a peanut butter and jelly sandwich for dinner.

"She can't stand PB and J anymore, Nimo," he said. "She's working a double today, she won't be home until real late anyway."

"Did you pass your test, Ate?" I asked him. He shrugged.

"Do you think you failed it?"

"It didn't seem too hard, but I'm not sure. It's one of those things where you just gotta wait it all out. I never told you about the time I found out Ina was gonna have you, right?" I shook my head and Ate kept on carving and told me the story.

"I was the temp janitor at Sioux Nation and Ina had been calling me all day, but I was so busy, I couldn't call her back. Then the intercom came on and the announcement said 'Thunderclap, clean up on aisle four and while you're there, you might as well get some diapers for the baby your wife's gonna have.'"

"Whoa, really?" I said. He nodded and put an arm around my shoulders.

"Your ina appeared in the aisle and asked me if I got her message," he said. "I fell backwards and knocked down a display of canned peaches. I was such a mess, I couldn't even think right. I was so scared, Nimo, but everything turned out better than we thought."

"I guess so," I shrugged. "Do you ever wish you would have waited to have me later, when you and Ina had more money?"

"If we waited until we had money, we still wouldn't have any kids," he said with a chuckle. "Your leksi and tunwinla have way more money than me and Ina and they only wanted one kid – can you believe that? I never had any second thoughts about you or Nellie. Hell, I could handle ten kids if Ina wanted that many. It was scary, Nimo, but the Creator takes care of us real good. With all the war and massacres our ancestors had, you would think we'd all be dead but here we are, thanks to the Creator. Now go make me a peanut butter and jelly sandwich, son, I'm starving." He blew the extra dust off his work in progress. I made a sandwich for Ate and one for myself. It was my third for the day.

On commodity day morning, Ate and me drank water for breakfast. Before we left for the office, the phone rang. He picked up and said, "How many times do I have to tell you people Jay Eagle Thunderclap is dead and can't make the minimum payment? Wait a second, what? Yeah, I'm Jay Eagle Thunderclap. No, I thought I was dead, but it turned out to be sleepwalking. Oh, all right. Thanks for calling."

"Who was it, Ate?" I asked, but he ran to the hallway and didn't hear me.

"I did it, Josie!" I heard him say from their bedroom. "I ain't stupid after all!" He carried Ina out to the living room and then he put her down and twirled her several times.

"Jay Eagle, you was never stupid," Ina said.

"It took me 17 years to finish high school," he said.

"If you was really stupid, you wouldn't have married me," Ina said and kissed his cheek. Ate blushed, like he always did every time Ina kissed him.

In the afternoon, I rode my bike to John David's house. There was a big rock on the street I didn't see and I flew into the dirt. Mrs. Graywolf drove past me. She stopped her truck and stepped out.

"Nimo, look at your knee," she said. She reached in her pocket, brought out a crumpled napkin, and put it over my knee.

"Thanks Mrs. Graywolf," I said. "It's not much blood."

"I can drive you to John David's, hoksila, I'm on my way to pick up Claudia from soccer practice – his house is on my route."

"How did you know I was going to John David's?"

"Where else would you be going?" she said with a smile. I put my bike in her truck's bed and she drove me down the street. Mrs. Graywolf had a picture of Claudia hanging from her rearview mirror. She was cute, but stuck up since her parents owned the most popular place on the rez. She wouldn't even eat her own ina's hot dogs because they were 'only 75 cents apiece.'

"Thanks for the ride, Mrs. Graywolf," I said when we got to John David's. "Tell Claudia I'll see her at school."

I parked my bike outside John David's house. He opened the door before I rang the bell, as usual.

"Hi Nimo," he said. "Everyone's talking about how your ate passed his test. Is he gonna get that job then?"

"Maybe," I shrugged. "They said they'd take him."

"If they don't hire him, we'll wrap the place in toilet paper," John David said.

"JD!" Miss Running Bear called from the backyard. "I'm going to Sioux Nation soon, do you need something? Diarrhea medicine?"

"Ina!" he said.

"I thought you might need it since you keep buying toilet paper with Nimo," she said as she walked inside the house. Miss Running Bear was short like Ina, but much thinner since

21

she liked to exercise and eat healthy food. John David and Miss Running Bear went for a run at dawn every day and ate at least one salad for a meal.

We ended up going to Sioux Nation with Miss Running Bear. John David and me skimmed through the snack aisle and he grabbed a giant bag of marshmallows and a box of graham crackers to make s'mores. When we got to the chocolate section, there was nothing on the shelf.

"I guess we can make marshmallow sandwiches," John David said. We went to find Miss Running Bear and we ran into my parents by the outdoor supplies. They were spinning hula-hoops around their waists.

"I'm gonna beat you," Ina said to Ate.

"Josie, you know I'm good with my hips," Ate answered. Shoppers crowded around and cheered them on. I waved to my parents and they waved back.

After John David and me ate our semi-s'mores, I rode my bike home in the dark. Ray Firebird suddenly leapt in front of me. I handed him a quarter.

"I heard your daddy passed his test," Ray Firebird said to me. "Give him my conjugations, okay?"

"Your what?" I said.

"My conjunctions," he said. "Tell him I said conductions on passing the test."

"I will," I said and pedaled away from him.

When I got home, Ate and Ina were snuggled together on the couch, watching a rerun of All in the Family. It was the one where Archie Bunker has to give a eulogy for his best friend's funeral, my favorite. I sat down to watch some of it with them.

"There's dinner on the table, Nimo," Ina said. "But please shower first."

After I was cleaned up, I went to the kitchen to heat up my food. I walked to the refrigerator to grab some water and when I swung the door open, all the shelves were full. I walked to the pantry and saw it as full as the refrigerator.

"I keep opening and closing the fridge because seeing all the food amazes me every time," Ate said. "Open the fridge again, son, I wanna see it one more time."

"You got the job?" I asked him.

"No, me and Ina robbed Sioux Nation at gunpoint," he said. "Yeah, I got the job and they gave me a check in advance for me to buy some tools, but it was enough to get some groceries. No more commod office. No more peanut butter and jelly sandwiches."

"No more telling the credit card people you're dead?" I said.

"Oh no, son, I've been dead for years, I can't just resurrect on them. Want some chocolate with your dinner?" I nodded. Ate sat down next to me and broke me off two big pieces of chocolate.

"I haven't eaten chocolate since Halloween," I said.

"Me either," Ate said. "I always eat your Halloween candy when you ain't looking. Why do you think you run out so fast?"

"Ate, that's not fair."

"Nimo, I used to change your diapers and give you baths when you smelled like hell, I deserve your Halloween candy," he said. He broke me off another piece of chocolate. We shared the bar until it was gone.

The Operation

My parents worked hard, but only when they could. They worked a lot to save up for a house and we got one in Cheyenne Estates. It wasn't very big. It was a small one story house with three bedrooms, but it also had a two car garage, a backyard, and a shed for Ate to keep his tools. Right when we were getting settled in, Ina lost her job at Shopping Cart.

"How can they lay off a janitor?" Ina said during dinner on the day she lost her job. "Who do they think is gonna clean the store? The mice?"

"I still got my job at Spotted Elk College and Nimo's got change in his piggybank, we'll be okay," Ate said.

"But what about your heart surgery, Ate?" I said as I picked at my broccoli. "It's next month."

"Don't worry, son, I'll just cut myself," he said.

"Jay Eagle!" Ina said and slammed her fork down on the table.

"What? I cut myself with my razor all the time, I think I can cut my chest open."

"Jay Eagle, you are having surgery and that's final. Even if we have to sell Nimo to the circus, you're doing it."

"The circus?" I said.

"We'll buy you back once we have enough cash," she said. "Eat your broccoli."

Ate was born with aortic valve stenosis. It means the valve that goes to his aorta doesn't open as big it should and his heart's blood flow isn't normal. It's like trying to drink a thick milkshake with a skinny straw – you have to drink harder and harder. The same goes for Ate's heart. His heart needed to work twice as hard as a normal heart. He had surgery for his stenosis when I was just a baby but the doctor said he needed surgery again. Now I was thirteen and Ate was still alive, even though he could die any second. I didn't like it when he took naps on the couch after dinner. I thought he might never wake up.

"Ate," I said one night as he napped during an All in the Family rerun. "Wake up, it's really late."

"Not now, Josie, I still got all my clothes on for crying out loud," he groaned. I nudged his shoulder with my hand and he turned to his left side.

"Josie, last thing I wanna do is knock you up after you've lost your job," he went on. "Go look at pictures of Sylvester Stallone."

"Ate, it's Nimo!" I said and he jolted up from the couch. He landed on the floor and he hit his head on the coffee table.

"Nimo! You could've given me a heart attack! What the hell is so important?"

"Sorry Ate," I said. "It's past midnight, Ina's in bed waiting for you."

25

"She is?" he asked with a big smile. "Then I shouldn't keep her waiting." Ate ran to the bedroom. I stayed on the couch watching the rest of the All in the Family episode until I fell asleep.

After two weeks, Ina still didn't have another job and Ate wanted to cancel his operation. They fell behind on the bills and we were back to eating peanut butter and jelly sandwiches for breakfast, lunch, and dinner. Peanut butter and jelly sandwiches are pretty good, but they're not when you eat them all day long.

"You're not cancelling your surgery," Ina said at breakfast one morning. "Can't your insurance cover the whole thing? What about the IHS Hospital?"

"It's only a percentage, we still gotta pay the two grand difference, Josie. I can live until we come up with it," he said. "I've gotten this far, what's a couple more weeks or months? I would do it with IHS, but Gray Mountain says Sioux Plains has better trained doctors or whatever. How hard can it be open up a valve? I open valves at work all the time."

"Wasn't I born at IHS?" I asked.

"You were," Ina said with a smile. "It was one hell of a birth, but they did it fine. Right, Jay Eagle? The doctors there are just fine."

"Fine? You were cussing them out while you were giving birth," Ate said.

"Well it hurt!" she said. "It really hurt because Nimo has your huge head!"

"You should've seen her, Nimo," he went on. "She cussed like a drunk sailor at those

doctors. She cussed at me, too. 'Damn you, Jay Eagle, I am

never letting you near me again!'"

"Get your head examined while you're at the hospital for your surgery," Ina said. The phone rang and Ate got up to answer.

"Whatever you're selling, we don't want it. Whatever you want, we don't care," he said. "Huh? Oh, you. No, you can't talk to Josie, she's dead. You can't talk to Nimo either, he's in jail for killing Josie."

"Who was it, Jay Eagle?" Ina asked after he hung up.

"Your ina," he said and Ina pulled on his ponytail.

After school, I went over to John David's house to work on our history project. We had to make a shoebox diorama about an event from the Civil War. We ended up choosing General Lee's surrender to General Grant at Appomattox Courthouse because it was the easiest one to make. We took some fat popsicle sticks and wrote General Lee and General Grant on them. Then we used brown construction paper and a cardboard jewelry box to make a desk. Our diorama was ugly, but it met everything Mr. High Hawk listed in the instructions.

"We're almost done, we only need to write the one-paragraph essay about the event," John David said while he glued a piece of construction paper that said "Lee Wusses Out" on the top of the shoebox. "I'll let you do that, you write better than I do."

"I already wrote it," I said and pulled it out of my backpack. "I guess we're done then."

"Awesome," he said as he stood up from his seat at the kitchen table. "C'mon, let's go to Big Bat's for a slushy. My ina gave me some money, I can pay for yours."

"No thanks," I said. "I love slushies, but I don't feel like it right now. I'm worried about my ate. He needs his surgery, but we're broke again."

"Oh yeah," he said and sat back down at the kitchen table. "I'm sure your parents will figure something out, they always do. My ate told me that before he had his restaurant, he used to eat raisins for dinner all the time. He figured something out and your ate will, too." I rubbed my face with my hands. John David was my best friend, my kola, but he didn't know what being broke felt like. It was hard to explain it to him. He always had everything he needed and even stuff he just wanted for fun. Being poor is a lot more than not having money – it's the fear that's the worst part. If we were rich, we wouldn't worry about Ate's surgery or that Ina lost her job or anything else. I always wondered what rich people worried about. It seemed to me like all their problems were covered since they could pay for them.

"It's hard when your parents don't have a lot of money," I said. "Every single day is scary. Sometimes I feel like we'll lose our house and go back to our trailer."

"It wasn't so bad from what I remember, it was smaller than your house, but it had everything you needed like a bathroom and a fridge."

"Yeah, I guess so. I'd rather never live there again though, it was falling apart and it was really small, way too small for me and my parents."

"You're lucky, Nimo," John David said. "I'd do anything to have both of my parents together again. I'd live in a box if I had to. My house in New York was way bigger than this one. I had a really big bedroom and a playroom with tons of toys just for me, but it didn't matter. Right before my parents split, they fought all the time. My ina slept in a room at the start of the hallway and my ate slept in a room at the end of the hallway.

I hated that so much, I used to sleep on the hallway floor to be closer to them. It sucked a whole lot. They had a bunch of stuff but they didn't have each other, you know?"

"Yeah," I said. "I know what you mean."

A couple days before Ate's surgery, Ina took me to the cash loan office just outside the rez. We waited in the lobby next to Ray Firebird.

"Hey Nimo," he said. "I thought you was in the slammer for killing your mother."

"He is, I need a loan to bail him out," Ina said. Ray Firebird nodded and pretty soon, he passed out on the floor, so we got to take his place when the clerk came out.

"I'm not sure we can give you a loan, Mrs. Thunderclap," the clerk told Ina. "Your credit score is substantially low and your household has 15 unpaid credit cards. I also see you purchased a house last year. Your debts are too high for another loan."

"Geez Ina, what did you need that many credit cards for?" I asked.

"To raise you," she said. The clerk shook his head and said Ina was better off paying for Ate's surgery with borrowed money from family.

"All of my family's broke, why the hell do you think I came here?" she said. The clerk grunted and gave Ina a sheet with the word DENIED in big letters.

For most of the drive home, Ina didn't say much. She kept scratching her head and twirling her earrings. We stopped at Big Bat's for lunch. Ina ordered chicken nuggets for me. She didn't get anything for herself, even though I could hear her stomach rumbling.

"Ina, what about Leksi Gray Mountain?" I said as I ate. "He's a doctor, I'm sure he'd let us borrow the money."

"You're right, Nimo," she nodded. "But Ate doesn't like asking his brother for cash. Oh, who cares what Ate thinks, he ain't even here. I'm gonna use the payphone outside, I'll be right back." I waited for her for about ten minutes. She came back, smiling. Leksi Gray Mountain said he'd send us a check, but not to tell Ate about it.

We got in the car and Ina drove back home. Ray Firebird stopped us right before we turned into our neighborhood's entrance. He waved his paper cup at Ina, asking her to spare at least a quarter.

"Ray, you know all I got to spare is one of my organs," Ina said. "Maybe I could spare this hoksila here and my husband too, but that's it."

"Ina!"

"I'm joking, if I gave you away, I'd tell you to take your ate with you."

"No change, Mrs. Thunderclap?" Ray Firebird said. "Not even a penny?"

"You got a penny to spare for the Thunderclap surgery fund?" Ina told him. She dug into her glove compartment and found a dollar. She handed it over to Ray Firebird. He slowly wobbled on to the next car. We finally parked in our driveway after a day that felt like it was a year long. Ate wasn't home yet – he was working an overtime shift to save some cash for his surgery. I hadn't seen him since dinner the night before and I missed him a lot.

"What do we tell Ate when he asks where the surgery money came from?" I asked Ina as we walked inside our house.

"Oh, he won't ask, he doesn't question money, especially at a time like this. What do you want for dinner tonight, Nimo?"

Ina said, looking at our almost empty panty. "We got some chicken, a can of soup, and some cereal. The Puentes are also in town this week. They always have good food to give away."

"Ina, we haven't seen them in a long time, they'll think we only liked them for their free stuff," I said.

"Well, to be honest, that is the reason why I liked them. It's their job," she said. "They'll understand. I never thought we'd see them again either for free stuff, at least not so soon."

On the day of Ate's surgery, we woke up super early to drive to the Sioux Plains Medical Center. I sat in the hospital waiting room with Ate and Ina. Ate squirmed in his seat so much, Ina whacked him on the head with a magazine.

"I'm about to get cut up and you're hitting me?" Ate said.

"Yeah, to knock you out so we won't have to pay for anesthesia," Ina said. Ate slouched in his seat. He stuck his tongue out at her. She shoved him away.

"Nimo, Josie," Ate said after a few minutes. "In the worst case scenario, after this surgery, I'll be dead. Nimo, you can have whatever I own which is nothing. Josie, if you meet another guy you really like, marry him."

"I already did years ago, he lives in our attic and he won't come downstairs until you croak," Ina said. She took hold of his hand. She didn't let go for a long time.

After Ate got called in, we waited for the doctor inside Ate's hospital room. He wore a big paper gown and wiggled all over the bed.

"Stop it, you'll break the bed," Ina said.

"If I wanted to break it, I'd bring you up here and make Nimo a sibling," he said. "I'm starving, I ain't eaten since yesterday. I guess it's good practice for how broke we're gonna be after this damn surgery."

"I'm hungry too, Ina," I said. "Can I have some change for the vending machine?"

"I'll run down to the deli to get a sandwich for you," Ina told me, patting my head. "If the doctor comes in while I'm not here, tell him to wait until I get back. I'll only be a few minutes. Okay, Nimo?"

"I'll tell him, Ina," I said. She kissed Ate on both of his cheeks before she left. I stayed at Ate's side, watching the presidential debate on the TV with him.

"Look at these guys," he said. "One's a bush, the other one's gore. Bush gore. Sounds like a haunted garden. I'll tell you something about politicians, they're like Mount Rushmore. They see you got a nice piece of land and they'll carve their faces into it permanently, especially if the land is sacred. They love sacred land."

"Is that why we've never gone to Mount Rushmore?" I asked.

"You ain't missing nothing except big stone faces and you can see stone faces at the annual Thunderclap family reunion."

"We've never gone to the reunions, Ate."

"Yeah, 'cause they're a bunch of stone faced rats. Plus, I ain't driving all the way to Rosebud rez just to hear, 'Jay Eagle! Whose son are you again?' Please, turn off the TV, Nimo, I can't take this debate anymore. If I wanted to hear an idiot talk, I'd call your unci." I shut the TV off and Ate slid further into the hospital bed. He was shaking, but he probably thought I didn't notice.

"Nimo," Ate said. "If I go, your ina will take good care of you. She always has. I'll be up in the sky with Nellie. Maybe she needs her ate to be with her right now."

"Don't say that, Ate, you're gonna be fine," I said.

"Just promise me two things if I don't make it out alive. First, keep my wedding ring. You pawn it and I'll come back from the dead and take you with me."

"I promise. What's the second thing you want me to do?"

"Second," he said. "Every single time your unci calls, heckle her." I laughed and we did a pinky swear.

"Son," he said. "I'm still paying the hospital bill for your birth. I told your ina to go to the backyard and squat when you was coming and she hit me. If she had squatted, we wouldn't have a bill for you."

"I didn't know that," I said with a frown. "I'm sorry, Ate. I have some leftover money from my birthday if you need it."

"You know," Ate said and tapped my shoulder. "I'm gonna miss you a lot if I go today. You're a great kid, Nimo. You're sweet, you're caring, and you're smart as hell. Nellie would have loved to have you as her tiblo."

Not long after, Ina was back with my sandwich and the doctor followed. He wheeled Ate away down the hall. I poked my head out the door, watching him leave.

"Remember those promises, Nimo!"

"I will, Ate," I said. "I love you."

Ina and me waited for Ate inside his hospital room. We played checkers, did some crossword puzzles, ate pretzels, and watched a couple reruns of Roseanne on the TV.

"I love this show," Ina said. "It was about time someone made a show about people like our family for a change."

"But didn't they get rich at the end anyway?"

"Those episodes don't count," she shook her head. "If we ever won the lottery, we'd share it with the rest of the rez. Everybody would know, no use in hiding the money. Ate would buy a new truck and I'd buy him a caller ID machine so he can stop bothering Unci."

"But Ina, it's funny when he does."

"Yeah, it is a little funny," she admitted. "This morning she called and he told her I was stuck inside Washington's ear at Mount Rushmore."

I grabbed the last pretzel and I peeked out into the hallway. No sign of Ate yet. It had already been around five hours and I didn't know how else to distract myself. I called John David from a payphone, but he couldn't talk for very long since he was helping his ina make some dinner for us. No matter what I did to distract myself, I couldn't stop thinking about Ate. I wanted to see him more than anything. Most of all, I wanted to hear him talk. I wanted to hear him say something funny, but at this point, even just hearing him say "hello" would be good enough. I knew some kids at school like George and Lorraine Ten Bears and Misty White Eyes who had two dads – their real dad and their stepdad. I imagined Ina remarrying if Ate did die and it made me sick. He was the only ate I wanted. The same went for Ina. I couldn't picture Ate being with anyone else and I couldn't picture myself having another person as my ina. I started to think about Ate dying and even Ina dying and it made me sick. I wish parents were immortal, but they're not. You only get them one time. When they're gone, that's it.

"Do you think Ate is okay, Ina?" I asked and sat down next to her. She flipped the pages in her crossword puzzle book to a blank one. She rubbed her wedding ring a few times.

"You're a big hoksila now," she said. "So I won't hide anything from you. Every surgery is scary, especially heart surgery. Ate's like a well-kept car – he can break down and get rusty, but he doesn't die. Worrying ain't gonna get you nowhere, Nimo.

Worrying is like carrying jacket with you in the Sahara desert because you think there might be a cold front. We could sit here and worry until it kills us or we can do something else to keep our minds busy. Now let's do this puzzle. Here, read the first clue."

"Row one, across, six letter word for a cat."

"That's easy, it's feline. We need to get harder puzzles than this junk," she said. Ina's eyes were as red as her lipstick.

"Did you get the job you applied for at Sioux Nation, Ina?"

"I don't know yet," she shrugged. "I would be doing the same thing I did at Shopping Cart. I'm tired of cleaning people's messes, hoksila. It's amazing how our people used to be fierce warriors and build up teepees and hunt buffalo. Now, we look for jobs like they're Easter eggs. That ain't what our ancestors died for. I don't care much for having a lot of money. I just want enough money to live a decent life with you and Ate."

"I hope you get the job, Ina."

"Me too, Nimo," she said. "You know, it's pretty funny, I ain't even thought about not having a job this whole day 'cause my mind's been on your ate. Problems get replaced by other problems, I guess."

Ate's surgery seemed to take the entire day. One of the surgeons stopped by the waiting room to tell us there was a small complication, but everything was fixed. Ate's breathing slowed down during the surgery and the doctors thought they were losing him. He breathed so slowly, it looked like he was about to die. Soon enough, he breathed normally again. Ina held her hand on her heart and she sighed "Thank you, Creator." The surgeon said the surgery was over, but they were keeping an eye on Ate for a while before taking him back to his hospital room.

"Do you think he's okay, Ina?"

"Nimo, he's fine," she said. "I have some blank paper in the back of this crossword puzzle book, you can write something if you want, get your mind on something else to feel better." I took the book from Ina and I found the blank pages she mentioned. Roseanne was still blaring on the TV, so I couldn't focus on writing very much. It was the episode where Roseanne yells at Dan for not fixing the sink while she was at work all day. Ina yelled at Ate too whenever he took forever to fix something at our house. A couple years back, when we lived in the trailer, we had a sink in our bathroom that wouldn't shut off all the way, a flickering porch light, and three weak floorboards in the kitchen. Ina begged Ate to fix everything, but he didn't. He said he couldn't. When she asked him why not, he said, "What do you think I am? Some kind of handyman?" Ina got so mad, she slammed her hands on the kitchen table and the table sunk into those weak floorboards.

"Look at that, Josie! You fixed the floor!" Ate said. "Go outside and slam your hands on the porch light while you're at it!"

"I feel like slamming my hands on your head to fix it!" Ina said. "You know how to fix all this broken stuff! You fix things at other people's houses, why can't you fix them at your own house? Last week, you replaced an entire floor at Nimo's school, then you fixed Mrs. Little Raven's flickering porch light, and then you fixed Mrs. Yellow Fire's dishwasher! What have you got to say about that, Jay Eagle?"

"Why don't we table this discussion?" Ate said and lifted the table off the broken floor. I couldn't help but laugh and neither could Ina. Eventually, Ate fixed everything, even the table. There was never a thing he couldn't fix.

An hour later, Ate was finally brought back into the hospital room, super high on anesthesia. He saw me first when he opened his eyes and he waved at me. He didn't recognize Ina though.

"Hey son," he said slowly and tapped my forearm. "Who's the burning hot nurse standing over there?"

"I'm your wife, you bonehead," Ina told him and kissed his cheek twice. "And this is our son, Nimo."

"What? You're my wife? And we got a son?" he said, half awake. "You mean, you married me and we've done it?"

"Yes, that's how we got our son," Ina said. I covered my face with my hands. If there was anything in life I didn't need to hear about, that was it.

"Awesome," Ate said. "Lady, you're the hottest nurse in the world. I should get surgery more often. You are smoking!"

"Jay Eagle, are you sure the doctor didn't take out your brain by mistake?" she said. "You need your head examined."

"Whatever you say, nurse. You can examine me anytime you want. If you need me to undress, I'll do that." He fell asleep and Ina adjusted the blanket over him.

"Nimo," Ina said. "Go home and tell my second husband in the attic to get lost."

The Clash

On Halloween afternoon, John David came over to my house to make masks out of paper bags because we didn't have money for a real costume. Since we were in 7th grade now, we felt too old to trick or treat, but not too old to have fun. In the end, we didn't look very threatening with our homemade masks.

"We look like blockheads," John David said.

"We're lunch bag phantoms," I said. We went to the porch to surprise Ate who was busy hanging up more decorations while Ina filled a bowl with assorted candy.

"Hey Josie!" Ate said when he saw us. "We've been invaded by blockheads!"

"Nimo, take that off, you'll suffocate," Ina said and pulled off my mask.

"Aw, c'mon, Ina," I said. "I wanna look scary for tonight."

"Then go find a picture of your unci and stick it on your face," Ate said.

"Do you have to make jokes about my ina every Halloween?" Ina asked.

"It ain't my fault she looks like a drugged up horse, Josie! Woman's so ugly, once the Creator was done making her, He slapped Himself."

"Now you listen here, you big bonehead!" Ina said. John David and me snuck inside while my parents went on bickering.

"Do you wanna try to make another mask?" John David asked.

"Nah, let's just scare them without one," I said.

"Maybe you can, you're ugly enough."

"Shut up, John David," I said.

We went back to the porch to give out candy right as Ate and Ina were going to the neighborhood block party in their biker costumes. They told us not to be too scary to the younger kids coming by.

"Isn't scaring people the point of Halloween?" I said.

"No, son," Ate said. "The point of every holiday is getting as much free food as you possibly can."

"Jay Eagle, you need your head examined," Ina said and tugged him away. John David and me waited for the kids to come and we had our paper bag masks on, but none of them got scared. They all laughed at us and called us blockheads.

"We should've gone to the party," John David sighed.

"I don't wanna hang out with my parents on Halloween," I said. "What do you say we go to Big Bat's?"

"To see Claudia Graywolf? She's pretty scary."

"No she's not, I think she's really cute. She's stuck up, but still cute."

"I think she looks like she got hit in the face with a shopping cart."

"John David, that's mean," I said as we got on our bikes. "The other day I heard at school that Claudia thinks you're cute. She wants you to take her to the winter dance."

"Me?" John David said with a big gasp. "Not a million years. Why don't you go with her? She makes me wanna puke."

We turned out of Cheyenne Estates and onto Fort Laramie Street. John David was always better looking than me, at least that's what I thought. I couldn't think of any girls at school who didn't have a crush on him, but he didn't care about any of them.

At Big Bat's, Claudia worked with Mr. Graywolf behind the hot dog counter. He was a vampire and she was a cat. Claudia had dark, curly hair I really liked. She never paid much attention to me though, probably since I was chubby. My crush was Cindy Blackbird anyway. I met Cindy at the Los Angeles Pow Wow earlier that year and no girl on Pine Ridge was prettier than her.

"Hi JD," Claudia said. "Is there anything special you'd like with your hot dog?"

"Uh," John David shrugged. "Chips."

"You like chips?" Claudia said, sounding way too excited. "What kind? Barbecue? I love barbecue chips! What about sour cream and onion?"

"Just give me a chocolate chip cookie, please," he said. We sat down at the far end of the dining area. Claudia kept her eyes on John David. She kept watch on him so much, she tripped and almost crashed into the slushy machine by the restrooms.

"Claudia really needs to get a hobby," John David said and took a bite out of his hot dog. "I can feel her eyes on my back."

"You don't think she's pretty at all?" I asked. "Not even a little?"

"I don't think she even needs a Halloween costume," he

answered. Claudia approached our table with wipes in her hand. She started cleaning the table, but she got too close to John David. He coughed on her to get her away. It didn't work.

"What a great cough, John David," she said.

"Claudia, for the Creator's sake, you're going to give the poor hoksila all your germs!" Mr. Graywolf said. "Wait until I tell Ina about this." Claudia finally backed off, but not without blowing a kiss to John David.

As we pedaled back to my house in the dark, John David said he thought a car was following us. I looked behind me and it was only Unci. We loaded our bikes on her car's rack and she asked us what we were doing out all by ourselves.

"Unci, we're in 7th grade," I said. "Ate and Ina let me go out whenever I want. Me and John David ate dinner at Big Bat's. We were just on our way home right now."

"Geronimo," Unci said and turned her face to me. She was the only person on the whole rez who called me by my real name. "It's terrible how your own ina lets you eat Big Bat's hot dogs almost every day. If we were living in the old days, you wouldn't make it as a warrior being so chubby. And don't you talk to me in English, that's not our ancestors' language."

"Sorry Unci, I forgot," I said in Lakota.

"I'm sorry too, Mrs. Red Cloud," John David said, also in his best Lakota.

I was Unci's only takoja, but I never felt very comfortable around her. She was always grumpy or angry. Whenever I was at her house, she'd make me speak to her only in Lakota and if I slipped in an English word on accident, she'd call me General Custer. She made really good frybread, but she would never let me have more than a mouthful. Everyone else's unci seemed sweet. They made cookies, bought toys, and stitched together blankets for winter. Mine didn't do any of that stuff. She usually stayed home all day and whenever she did come outside, she would either insult people or give them the middle finger if her throat was sore.

Unci pulled up to my driveway and Ina was at the door, waving to us. Ina and Unci went inside and John David and me stayed on the porch to have some leftover candy. Soon after, Ate came home carrying multiple plates.

"I got tons of food," he said. "I could've gotten more, but your ina said I was embarrassing her." He looked in his pocket for his keys and couldn't find them. He rang the bell instead. Unci swung the door open.

"Ah!" Ate shouted. "It's hideous!"

"Shut up!" Unci said.

"It talks too!" Ate screamed. "Quick Nimo, get the garlic!" Ina shoved Ate inside. She slammed the door so hard, the porch shook. Some of our neighbors peeked out their windows to see what was going on.

"Nimo, how come your ate and unci are always fighting?" John David asked. I told him I heard it was because Unci didn't want Ina to marry Ate and she always brought it up. Then Unci came out of the house. She stomped her feet on the porch.

"I don't care who Josie was engaged to before, she married me!" Ate shouted at her. "When I proposed, she didn't have to say yes, but she did! And I don't give a shit what you think about me, Sequoia, you're an old, delusional, horse-faced hag!"

"Jay Eagle," Unci said. "Josie was supposed to marry Eric White Feather, a lawyer with his own practice in Sioux Plains, his own practice! If Geronimo's dad was Eric White Feather, he'd be perfect, but he's just like you! He talks like you, he acts like you, he looks like you, and I hate it!" Unci walked past me, jumped into her car, and sped off. Ate's eyes met up with mine. He didn't say anything – he just shook his head.

Unci didn't come to our house and we didn't go to hers for weeks. She lived in Wounded Knee, not far from Cheyenne Estates. It was the same house Ina grew up in and it was falling apart. Ina visited Unci every Sunday afternoon, usually dragging me or Ate with her, but not anymore.

The Sunday before Thanksgiving, Ate was on the porch, carving another pipe. I went outside to watch him work. Snow covered the beat up streets and more kept falling down. He had a little fire going next to him to keep warm.

"Ate," I said and sat down. "How come Unci doesn't like me?"

"Don't be ridiculous, she loves you," he said and smoothed the edges of the pipe.

"She said I'm just like you," I reminded him.

"Yeah," Ate said. "That means she don't like me, not you." I tightened my jacket and stuck my hands in the pockets. Icy air shot out of my mouth.

"Is it true Ina was supposed to marry someone else?"

"Not really," he said and set his knife aside. "When I met Ina, she had just broken off her engagement to Eric White Feather. He was a lawyer, had his own office, a new car, a house, but he liked to drink. He was older than her, I think about ten years older, maybe a little less than that. Anyway, one night, a couple days after he proposed, he took Ina to Rapid City for the weekend to celebrate. Instead of celebrating with her, he spent the whole weekend getting wasted at a bar. Ina found him and she said, 'I'm breaking off this engagement.' Then he broke a beer bottle and sliced Ina's neck. That's how she got her big scar. After that night, she never saw Eric again and didn't want to. Just because she was engaged, it didn't mean she had to marry him. Fast forward a couple weeks later, me and Ina meet for the first time and here we are today.'"

"So, Unci doesn't like me because Eric White Feather's not my ate."

"Nimo," Ate sighed. "When you was six months old, you caught a fever and it wouldn't go down and our car's battery died. Unci came over, covered you in her big, red coat and took you to the ER. She stayed up with you for two whole days."

Wolf Creek School was closed for Thanksgiving break. I spent most of my time at John David's house, playing video games and watching Roseanne reruns. John David said Claudia somehow got his phone number. Every time she called, he made up an excuse so he wouldn't have to talk to her for very long.

"This morning, I told her I couldn't talk because I accidentally set my hair on fire," he said. "Next time she calls, I'll tell her I set my ear on fire and I can't hear her."

"She's not so bad," I said. "All the girls at school like you, John David, you might as well go out with one of them."

"No way!" he said, jumping backwards. "I'd rather watch paint dry than go out with the girls at our school." I thought John David was out of his mind. If I looked like him, even Claudia would want to go out with me. Cindy would probably ask me to marry her as soon as we graduated from high school. John David never talked about girls much. They sure talked about him though. When it came to me, all the girls called me "John David's fat friend."

"Do you like girls, John David?" I asked him during a

commercial break from Roseanne. He looked at me with an open mouth.

"Do I like girls?" he said, almost laughing. "Uh, yeah, of course I do. Girls are, they're girls. Girls, girls, girls being girly girls."

"I better head home, it's almost dinnertime," I said and stood up. "Are you and your ina coming over tomorrow for Thanksgiving?"

"Yeah, we'll be there around noon. My ina wants to help out with the cooking," he said and walked me to the door. "Oh, and Nimo, I love girls. I love them so much, I'd marry ten of them at the same time if I could, but I can't because that's wrong, I think."

"Okay," I said with a shrug. "I was just asking. See you tomorrow." Outside, the snow started falling hard again. I only lived two streets up from John David, but I was frozen when I reached my house. A load of snow landed on Ate's truck, so much I couldn't see inside the windows.

"Hey there, hoksila," Ate said when I walked inside. "Wanna watch some Roseanne with me? This is the one where Roseanne and Dan go to Las Vegas."

"No thanks, Ate, I'm really hungry," I said. Ina was in the kitchen, making a list of everything she planned to cook for Thanksgiving. Hot chocolate boiled in a pot on the stove. Frybread sat on a plate right next to it. I got a mug of hot chocolate and some bread. Finally, I felt warm again.

"I don't know how I'm going to cook dinner this year," Ina said. "There are so many things for me to buy. Ever since I started working at Sioux Nation, I haven't had time to do any of the shopping!"

"Or do anything else, Josie!" Ate said from the living room

over Roseanne's blaring voice. "If you know what I mean!"

"Shut up or I'll serve you for Thanksgiving dinner!"

About an hour later, we bundled ourselves up and went to Sioux Nation. Ate dropped Ina off at the front of the store and we searched for a decent place to park. We went around in circles, so Ate gave up and parked in an expectant mothers spot.

"Ate, we're not pregnant," I told him with my teeth chattering.

"Like hell we ain't," he said and rubbed his stomach. "Move it, Nimo, one more minute out here and I'm gonna be colder than your unci's heart."

Ate went to look for Ina and I went my own way. While I browsed the snack aisle for some trail mix, I felt a big bump on my leg from a shopping cart. I turned my head. It was Unci. She looked at me and ran out from the aisle.

"Unci, wait!" I said. I followed behind her, but she left her cart aside and went inside the women's restroom. I stayed by the restroom, waiting for her to come back out. She never did.

On Thanksgiving Day, John David and Miss Running Bear came over right at noon. Ate was in the garage, grilling the turkey, and blasting Judas Priest on his handheld radio. We offered to help him, but he wouldn't let us.

"Hoksilas, I don't let anyone learn my grilling secrets," he said over the music. "Not even Mrs. Thunderclap knows what kind of spices I use!"

"Jay Eagle, turn that down! I'm losing my hearing!" Ina shouted from inside. Ate turned the music up even louder.

"Happy Thanksgiving, hoksilas!" Ate yelled.

Leksi Gray Mountain and Tunwinla Rosa came over around five o'clock with Lucille. While the adults talked in the kitchen,

John David and me played with Lucille in the living room. She asked me if I could give her a piggyback ride, but I wasn't sure I was strong enough, especially since she had grown so much.

"Why don't you ask John David?" I told her.

"He's not my sicesi! You're my sicesi, Nimo!" she said.

"Yeah, Nimo, I'm not her cousin. Give her a piggyback ride, you jerk," John David said. She started to cry, so I picked her up, put her on my shoulders, and walked around the living room while she used my head as a drum.

"Lucy, stop it," I said. "You're hurting me."

"I love you, Nimo!" she said and wrapped her tiny arms around my forehead. "I wish you were my tiblo!"

"And I love you!" I said. I took her off my shoulders and raised her up in the air. She wasn't Nellie, but she was the closest thing I had to a thanksi.

Before dinnertime, John David and me snuck into the kitchen to steal some of Ina's famous dinosaur shaped chocolate chip cookies. John David wrapped a couple in a napkin for us, but Ina caught him and grabbed them from his hands. The doorbell rang and Ina looked confused. Ate put his eye on the door's peephole.

"Who is it, honey?" Ina asked.

"It's just the bride of Frankenstein, sweetie, I'll get the shotgun," Ate said. Ina swung the door open and Unci barged inside.

"I was supposed to go to the Thanksgiving party at the senior center," Unci said. "But the guy who organized it had a heart attack and it was cancelled."

"I should have faked a heart attack too," Ate whispered. Ina pulled his ponytail and led Unci to a chair far away from Ate.

"Hey Gray Mountain," Ate said. "Is that a white hair on your head?"

"Yeah, it showed up last week," Leksi said, rubbing his scalp. "I am 40 now. It was going to come sooner or later. And, I've been married for six years."

"You've been married six years and you got one white hair?" Ate said. "Watch out when you've been married 14 years. Your black hair's gonna drop out faster than the kids at our old high school."

"Jay Eagle, if you hate being married so much, you shouldn't have married my daughter," Unci said. The entire table went quiet, except for Lucille, who was asking me for some macaroni and cheese.

"Josephine, if you really wanted to be a Thunderclap, you should've married Gray Mountain," she said. "He's a doctor, not a lousy handyman like Jay Eagle."

"Handymen are good, Leksi can't fix anything," Tunwinla Rosa said. "Well, he fixes sick people, so he's kind of a handyman, too."

"He's a better handyman than Jay Eagle," Unci said.

"Ina, please," Ina said. "Just eat something. There's plenty of food."

"I can't eat with Jay Eagle in my face, he makes me want to throw up," Unci said. Ate stood up from his seat, walked into the kitchen, and came back with our broom. He placed it in Unci's hands.

"I thought you might need this for your flight home," Ate said. Unci raised a fist at him. She waved it in his face.

"Would anyone like some more mashed potatoes?" Miss Running Bear asked. "Me and Josie used the best butter, the $1.99 kind. John David, why don't you tell us about Claudia? She's been calling you all week."

"Ina!" John David said and picked at his turkey slices. "I'm trying to eat here! I don't wanna talk about girls!"

"Jay Eagle, you have been my son in law for over 14 years now and I've hated every single minute of it," Unci said. She rose up from her seat to point at him.

"Lucille can count to 20 now!" Tunwinla Rosa said. "Show us, Lucy, show us."

"Yes, Lucy, count for us," Ina said. Lucille didn't count though. Unci and Ate left the table to carry on their fight in the kitchen. They closed the door, but we still heard them clearly. I heard Unci call Ate half a man and he told her she was so ugly, she could go to Mount Rushmore and crack all the president faces off the hill just by looking at them. I never liked the way Unci talked to Ate. She didn't know Ate as well as anyone else did and it's not like she ever tried to get to really know him anyway. If she did know him, I was sure she would like him, maybe not love him, but she would like him.

"Mrs. Thunderclap, can me and Nimo be excused?" John David asked. Ina nodded and we rushed to my room.

"I thought there was gonna be a food fight soon," John David said. He sat down on the floor and turned on my TV to an episode of All in the Family.

"I wish I could've eaten more," I said. "I didn't even get any of the dino cookies."

"Don't worry, I stuck some in my pocket," he said and handed me one.

"Didn't my ina take those from you?"

"Yeah, but I took them back when she wasn't looking."

"Where'd you learn to steal food like that, John David?"

"Your ate. Remember how he snuck out a piece of cherry pie from Betty-O's Buffett when we went there for your ina's

49

birthday? He put it in your unci's purse and she didn't notice until we got home 'cause it came apart and stained her whole purse red!" We laughed, unlike the rest of the house that Thanksgiving.

A couple days before Christmas, there was a block party at the Yellow Fire house, our neighbors across the street. Nobody in my immediate family was a Christian. We were one of the families who stuck with the traditional Lakota religion. But when it was Christmastime and there was a party with free food, we always showed up.

"Hurry up, Josie!" Ate called from the living room. "By the time you're ready, it'll be New Year's Day!"

"One second, I'm putting on my face!" she said.

"Ate, what does she mean when she says that?" I asked.

"Son, your ina's real face fell off years ago. She never got it replaced. She wears a mask so she don't scare people."

"Ate, c'mon," I said.

"Really, Nimo," he said. "Her mask is made out of a paper bag. She irons it every night before we go to bed."

"Jay Eagle, how many times do I have to tell you to stop putting Nimo's mind in the garbage?" Ina said. "Everyone knows my face mask is made out of a plastic bag."

When we got to the block party, Ate was already stuffing food into Ina's purse. I saw John David having a mug of hot chocolate in the corner and I went to join him. Before I got to him, Claudia stepped in.

"You like hot chocolate too, John David?" she asked him. "I love hot chocolate! What kind is your favorite? Mine is the double chocolate kind. What's yours? Tell me and I'll see if we have some at Big Bat's." I made eye contact with John David.

He winked and spilled some of his hot chocolate on his shoe.

"Whoops! Look like I burned my foot!" he said. "Sorry Claudia, gotta go dip my foot in the snow outside!" John David stepped out. I started walking after him, but Claudia stopped me.

"What is with your friend?" she said. "Does he think he's too good for me?"

"No," I said. "John David's just really accident prone. I'm surprised he's still alive to be honest with you."

"He needs to work on that," Claudia said. "You're not so bad yourself, Nimo, but you seriously gotta drop some pounds."

I joined John David outside at last. We sat on the Yellow Fire's porch. Miss Running Bear arrived with some more of her fresh fruit salad. She told us to get inside because it was too cold to be out.

"Claudia," John David said. "Claudia, Ina."

"Oh, she's a nice girl," Miss Running Bear said as she went inside the house. "She only likes you because you look cute like I do. Get your butt off this stone cold porch before you turn into a walrus."

"Nimo, are there any more dino cookies at your house?" John David asked. "Ray Firebird came over earlier and he ate them all."

"Yeah, I'll get some just for us," I said. "I'll meet you by the fireplace inside." I ran across the street in the heavy snow and when I got to the door, I dropped my house key through a hole in the porch. I climbed underneath the porch stairs, but I got stuck. No matter how hard I tried to wiggle out, I only got more stuck.

"Someone help me!" I called out. "I'll give you a cookie!" After a few minutes, I felt a hand tug on my legs, pulling me. I slipped out at last.

"Unci?" I said when I got up. "What are you doing here?"

"My unci senses told me my chubby takoja was going to get stuck under his porch tonight," she said. Unci climbed under the porch stairs and grabbed my house key. We ran inside to warm up. She wore her big, red coat.

"Geronimo," she said as I put some dino cookies in a plastic container. "I've been meaning to talk to you, but I didn't know if you wanted to talk to me."

"I did, Unci," I said. "But I thought you didn't like me." I offered her a dino cookie and she shook her head, maybe because of her diabetes. She told me to sit down by her. She held me close as she lightly stroked my hair.

"Geronimo," she sighed. "I know me and your ate fight like crazy, but I don't hate him, not one bit."

"You don't?" I said. "I thought you were gonna kill him on Thanksgiving."

"Oh, no," Unci said. "If it wasn't for him, you wouldn't be here. When I found out your ina was gonna have a baby, I asked the Creator to give me the best takoja ever and I got my wish. You're just like your ate, but it's okay. Your ate's a good man. He's a good husband and he's a good ate to you. But don't ever tell him I said that."

"How come?" I asked.

"Because then he'll talk to me," she said. "Let me tell you a story, hoksila. When you were born, I wasn't on the rez. I went with your tunkasila all the way to Sante Fe, New Mexico for the wedding of some distant relative of his, I don't even remember who it was. Anyway, I didn't wanna go because you were due any second and Santa Fe is almost 700 miles away but he begged me to go. Right when we got to the wedding, we got a call from IHS saying our daughter was having her baby and if we didn't leave right away, we'd miss the birth. We jumped in our car and drove like maniacs back to Pine Ridge."

"Did you make it back to Pine Ridge in time?" I asked.

"Just barely," she said. "When we got to IHS, I heard your ina screaming in pain. She pushed one more time and you were finally out. A minute later and your tunkasila and me would've missed everything. Your ate let me hold you when you were just a couple minutes old. I told him, 'he's got my eyes.' Your ate said 'so what? He's got my last name.'"

"Ate would say something like that," I said with a smile. "Uh, since we're talking about him, he's never wanted to stop me from seeing you. He might say you're ugly, but he has never called you a bad unci."

"That's nice to know, Geronimo," Unci said. "Thank you. Now let's get to the party before Ray Firebird eats all the food."

I tucked the container of cookies under my right arm. Unci took off her scarf, put it around my neck, and we raced to the Yellow Fire house through more falling snow.

The Vacation

When my parents reached their 16th wedding anniversary, I thought they'd go on a weekend trip to Sioux Plains and I'd have the house to myself. But instead, they decided on a trip to Rapid City and they wanted to drag me with them.

"Why are you taking me? Don't you need your romance?" I said at breakfast.

"Nimo," Ina said. "We've been married for 16 years now. We have no romance."

"You'll have fun," Ate said and poured syrup all over his plate. "We're gonna visit the National Carpet Museum, take a tour of a laundromat, and if we have enough time, a visit to the cement factory."

"Jay Eagle, you're ridiculous," Ina said. "We are going to the manure factory."

"That's fun too, son," Ate said. "They let you bring back some manure as a souvenir. You can ask John David if he wants to come with us." I put my hands over my face and groaned while they laughed at me.

"It won't be so bad," Ina said. "I'm sure you'll have some fun."

After breakfast, I got on my bike and pedaled to John David's house. He was in his driveway, putting some new handlebars on his bike. I stepped in to help and while we got all greased up, I asked if he wanted to go to Rapid City with me.

"If I wanted to see some manure, I could go Big Bat's and look at Claudia."

"John David, you know my parents aren't serious most of the time," I said. "Geez, I hope they aren't being serious this time."

"I guess we should go, Nimo," he shrugged. "It might be the most exciting thing we get to do all summer. I'll ask my ina about it tonight."

John David was at my house by 7:30am the next day. We each had three bowls of marshmallow cereal and Ate got mad at us for not saving any for him.

"I thought Ina said you couldn't eat this kind," I said.

"Ina's in the shower," he said and munched on the last of the cereal in the box. Ate was a strong man at five feet nine inches and 240 pounds. He gained a lot of weight over the years, but he could run, do backflips, and lift up anything heavy. I didn't like it when he ate unhealthy food though. His aortic valve stenosis could get him any second.

"Jay Eagle, did you eat the junk cereal?" Ina said while brushing her hair.

"No, I had SuperFiberMan," he said and leaned against the kitchen counter. Ina shook her head at him.

"There's a mini marshmallow on your cheek," she said and brushed it off. "You are so stubborn, Jay Eagle. What about your heart?"

"If my heart's ever gonna burst, it's gonna be because of you," Ate told her and pressed his cheek against her nose. "You make it go crazy when you're close to me."

"Oh, get your cooties off me," Ina said and lightly shoved him.

We were on our way to Rapid City by 8:15 in the morning. For most of the drive, Ate blasted Judas Priest, Black Sabbath, and Twisted Sister. Ina constantly screamed "turn that down," but he turned it up even louder. When we got to Rapid City two hours later, Ina said she wanted to go to Dinosaur Park.

"Josie, if I wanted to see a giant meat eating lizard, I could've gone to your ina's house," Ate said and Ina pulled on his ponytail. Ate turned the car towards Dinosaur Park. I hadn't been to Dinosaur Park since I was four. I remember crying because I was scared of the T-Rex. Ina tried to calm me down by telling me dinosaurs weren't real anymore. Ate made growling sounds and lunged at the T-Rex.

"I killed him, son," he said. "Ate-saurus came to the rescue." For the rest of our trip, I couldn't stop crying because I thought Ate was a dinosaur killer. Ina bought dinosaur shaped cookie cutters at the gift shop and when we got home, she made me dino cookies for the first time.

"Here we are, everyone," Ate announced when we arrived. "Don't worry, Nimo. I won't kill any of the dinos this time."

"Ate, I'm 14," I said.

"I'm 39," Ate said. "How old are you, Josie? 100?"

"Jay Eagle, you need your head examined," Ina said and stepped out of the car. Ate and Ina went in one direction while John David and me went our own way. We found the T-Rex just as I remembered him – big, green, and showing his sharp teeth.

"He's smiling, Nimo," John David said. "That's not scary at all."

"He's huge and green and he's got tiny arms, that's pretty scary," I said.

"So does Ray Firebird," he said and I laughed. We went to check out the rest of the park, but when we got to the Stegosaurus, we found Ate and Ina kissing.

"That's so gross, why do they have to do that?" I said.

"It's no big deal," John David said. "Everyone makes out."

"They make out everywhere. The other day, we were at Big Bat's filling up my ate's truck and they made out there too."

"It doesn't bother me," John David said. "I never saw my parents kiss." During the rest of our time at the park, Ina held Ate's hand, like she always did when they were out in public. She put her head on Ate's chest and they swayed from side to side.

The next day, we ate an early lunch at Arnold's Diner before heading to the Journey Museum. There was a Lakota Sioux exhibition Ina wanted to check out.

"Josie, we live on Pine Ridge, we are a Lakota Sioux exhibition," Ate said. But Ina got tickets anyway and we went inside. When we were by a teepee display, a lady asked Ate how big our teepee was.

"Oh, it's very, very big," Ate said. "In fact, it's about as big as the hole in your brain." The lady stormed off, muttering something to herself. She seemed really disappointed about us not living in a teepee.

We looked around some more and we didn't see anything new or interesting about being Lakota. The exhibition had a couple artifacts like arrowheads, drums, and headdresses, but not much else. According to the exhibition's outdated pamphlet, we still lived in teepees, dressed in buckskins, and hunted buffalo when we were hungry.

"Josie, can we get out of here?" Ate said. "This place is a joke. If these people wanna see some real Lakota Indians, they can just drive two hours to Pine Ridge."

"You are such a baby," Ina said and walked towards the exit with Ate making baby sounds behind her.

On our way back to Pine Ridge, we stopped at a small gas station in Hermosa for snacks. John David and me headed straight to the trail mix.

"Can I get cookies, Josie?" Ate asked. "Cookies that aren't SuperFiberMan?"

"Jay Eagle, if you want some sugar, you can just tell me," Ina said and gave him a kiss on his lips. He blushed deeply. We picked out our snacks and stood in line with an impatient man behind us who kept telling the cashier to work faster. The register's credit card machine crashed and they were only taking cash. When it was our turn, Ina searched through her purse for spare change.

"Jay Eagle, don't you carry cash?" she asked Ate. "I think I used all of mine at the stupid museum."

"C'mon now, some of us don't have all day long to stand here!" the man behind us said. "Let's move it!"

"I only have a five dollar bill, baby," Ate said.

"Oh, we're still sixty cents short," she answered. "I think there's some change in the truck, I'll go check really quick."

"Hey lady!" the man said. "People are waiting!"

"I'm so sorry, sir, go right ahead," Ina told him and stepped out of the line.

"Damn dirty Indian don't know where her money is!" the

man shouted to everyone in the store. "These goddamn Indians, it's a goddamn shame Custer didn't get all of you when he could!" John David and me looked at each other. The rest of the gas station was quiet. I heard from Leksi Gray Mountain how Ate used to get in fights as a teenager. He told me Ate broke noses, blackened eyes, and twisted arms. I was pretty scared for what could happen next. Ate grabbed the man by his shirt collar and dragged him outside, but everyone could see the fight through the glass window. Ate punched the man several times, hard enough to make him bleed from his mouth.

"You hate Indians? Then guess what? I'm gonna scalp you and hang your hair up in my living room, you son of a bitch!" Ate screamed at the man. "Then I'm gonna cut your face off and wipe my ass with it!" I thought Ina would tell Ate to stop, but she ran outside to cheer for him. The man swung some punches back at Ate. He wasn't as strong as Ate, luckily.

"Okay, you made your point!" the man said. He jumped into his car and sped away, still bleeding from his mouth.

A week after our Rapid City vacation, everyone on the rez knew about the fight. Ate got a letter from the state of South Dakota. He was being sued by Tom Hughes, the man from the gas station fight. Someone who saw the fight got Ate's license plate, told Tom, and Tom called the police. Ate had the choice of going to court in Rapid City or paying a $2,000 fine.

"We got some money in the savings account," Ina said.

"Since when do we have a savings account, Josie?"

"Since we got married and got our parents' inheritances," Ina said and Ate groaned. I told them I was going to hang out with John David, but they didn't hear me since they were still talking about Ate being sued.

I rode my bike to John David's house and soon after we went to Big Bat's for lunch. During our ride there, Ray Firebird jumped in front of us.

"Hey Nimo, I hear your daddy got in a fight with ten guys at a bar in Rapid City," he said, with breaks in between each word.

"Uh," I said. "Yeah, he sure did."

"Really? I heard he fought them all with a bowl of peanuts."

"Sure did," I said and gave him fifty cents so we could keep on riding.

At Big Bat's, people kept telling me the stories they heard. The stories went from Ate fighting three guys with a tennis racket to Ate bashing a seven foot tall man's face in with a pineapple.

"I didn't know your ate was so violent, Nimo," Claudia said to us while we waited on our hot dogs. "I hope he washed his hands after fighting that guy, he didn't even know where he's been. You went too, didn't you, John David? Don't you think violence is wrong and never okay? Don't you? Don't you?" Claudia asked him. Mr. and Mrs. Graywolf looked at Claudia with raised eyebrows.

"Me?" John David said, nervously. "No, I love violence. Violence should be given out like hot dogs, right Nimo?"

"I'll take some violence instead of potato chips with my hot dog," I said. Claudia stuck her tongue out at us.

"Typical," Claudia said. "All boys are the same."

"Ain't that the truth," Mrs. Graywolf said. Mr. Graywolf made the raspberry sound with his tongue.

When I got home for dinner, I saw Ate at the kitchen table. He clicked the buttons on a calculator and cussed out loud.

"Hi Ate," I said and opened up a bag of chips.

"Put those chips away, son, your ina left you some pot roast in the fridge."

"What are you doing, Ate?"

"I'm spelling BOOBS on the calculator, hoksila," he grunted. "I'm trying to figure out how the hell we're gonna pay for this fine." Right then, Ina walked inside carrying three paper bags from Sioux Nation.

"The cashier gave me a 15 percent discount on top of my employee discount since he heard my husband fought 15 guys with a can of Sioux Nation peaches," Ina said as she put the groceries down on the kitchen table.

"Dammit Josie, I beat the guy up for you!" Ate said.

"I know, sweetie," Ina said and squeezed his cheeks. "But you cost us $2,000."

"Me? You're the one who wanted to go to Rapid City and you're the one who wanted to stop at that damn gas station!" Ate said. "I wanted to go to Omaha, but you thought Nimo would burn the house down because you think he's still a baby!"

"That's because he is a baby, Jay Eagle," Ina said. "I wanted him to be safe with us, but excuse me for trying to be a good mother to our son!" The phone suddenly rang and Ate picked it up before Ina or me could.

"What the hell do you want, you loser? Sorry, I don't speak baboon!" Ate said and then put the phone back on the hook. "Dammit, Josie, can't your ina call when I'm not home?"

"Don't you say another word about her, Jay Eagle!" Ina shouted at him. Soon enough, they were fighting about whose fault it was that the fight happened. I heated up my pot roast and slipped away to my room as they kept screaming at each other.

For a couple of days, Ate and Ina barely spoke to each other and when they did, it usually ended with one of them yelling. Ate kept saying he could talk his way out of paying since Tom used hate speech, but Ina said if he ended up in jail, she would too.

"What the hell is that supposed to mean, Josie?" Ate said.

"If you go to jail, I'm going too 'cause I'll beat your face in for leaving me alone. I'll do it with a can of Sioux Nation peaches too! Then Nimo can beat both of us with the canned peaches and we'll all be in jail together like one, big, happy family!"

"I don't wanna beat you up, Ina!" I said. "Or you, Ate!"

"You're gonna have to if Ina has her way," Ate said. "Go play with John David or something, hoksila, this is gonna take a while."

I rode my bike to John David's even though he had a cold and couldn't come outside. We watched Roseanne reruns on TV until close to lunchtime.

"I'm hungry," I said. "Do you think you can go to Big Bat's with me?"

"No," he shook his head. "I don't feel good. Sorry, Nimo."

"Is Claudia still calling you?"

"Yeah," he sniffled. "At least now I'm really sick and I'm not lying to her."

"Are you starting to like her? She's kinda cute, you know."

"Not to me," he said. "I heard Scott Black Bear likes her. When I get better, I'll see if I can set them up or something."

"What?" I asked. "You're gonna pass a cute girl onto Scott? Toilet Paper Scott?"

"Sure," he said. "I don't like her, so why not?"

After having a bite at Big Bat's by myself, I pedaled to Spotted

Elk College to visit Ate. The college was big on the outside and even bigger on the inside. There were staircases, wide hallways, and tons of classrooms. It looked like a nice place to work and a nice place to go to school. I walked around for a while and eventually I bumped into Noe Black Bear, Ate's assistant, by the restrooms.

"You looking for your daddy?" Mr. Black Bear asked. "He's fixing a water fountain by the library. Take the elevator to the third floor."

"Thanks Mr. Black Bear," I said.

"No problem, Nimo," he said. "Is it true your dad beat up four guys with a mop?"

"It was six guys with a sponge," I said and headed to the third floor. Ate banged on the broken water fountain with his wrench, cursing at it.

"You son of a bitch, I'm gonna rip you off the floor and throw your broke ass out the window like in One Flew Over the Cuckoo's Nest!" he said to the water fountain. He kept mumbling curse words until he saw me standing behind him.

"Nimo, you almost gave me a heart attack," he said. "What are you doing here?"

"John David's sick," I said. "Why do you and Ina keep fighting? Don't you like each other anymore?"

"Of course we do," Ate said and got back to fixing the water fountain. "I think."

"Are you gonna go to jail?" I said. Ate put his wrench down.

"No, of course not," he said. "Hate speech is hate speech. I'll win the case."

"Good," I said. "If you went to jail, that'd suck because you got a bad heart and I really want you around for as long as possible."

"Aw Nimo," Ate said, putting an arm around me. "I'm not gonna die until it's my time to go. And, I need to show you where the Thunderclap family fortune is hidden."

"Oh yeah? Where is it?" I asked.

"Hell, I don't know, I'm still looking for it," he said. "Tell Ina I'll be home a little late today on account of this damn water fountain."

"I will, Ate," I said. He gave me a long hug. I slowly walked away from him, hearing him curse at the water fountain.

When I got home, it was past dinnertime, but Ina hadn't cooked since she was exhausted from her work shift. She was resting on the couch with an All in the Family episode blasting from the TV.

"Ina, I'm starving," I whispered. "Can I have cereal for dinner?"

"Nimo, Ate just went to get burgers from Big Bat's. You'll live."

"What if I die of starvation?" I said.

"Then me and Ate will sell your corpse to the slaughterhouse and use the money for a vacation to Disneyworld. What did you do today?"

"I went to John David's," I said. "And then to Big Bat's for lunch, Ate's job, and I used the payphone at Sioux Nation to call Cindy. She misses me a whole lot."

"Why wouldn't she?" Ina said with a smile. "You're so cute."

"Ina, can I talk to you about something?" I said. She nodded and put an arm around me. Ate finally walked in with a bag of hot burgers, fries, and sodas.

"Why did that man call you a dirty Indian?" I asked her.

"Because that man is a no good, damn son of a bitch and the

biggest motherf--"

"Jay Eagle!" Ina said. "If you need to curse, at least do it outside, not in front of Nimo. We're talking here."

"Josie, I'm hungry, I ain't eaten since breakfast this morning."

"We won't be long, honey, I promise. Once we're done talking, we'll have dinner. I'll even make you some brownies if you want."

"All right, I'll go curse at the grass," he said and went to relax on his hammock in the backyard.

"Okay, Nimo," Ina went on. "He called me that because there are people who really don't like Indians. He's one of them."

"You mean, people still don't like us?" I said. "After all this time?"

"Nimo," Ina said. "The Creator wants us to be nice to everyone, even when they're not nice to us first. We're Lakota and some people out there might not like that about us. But we're also good people and good people can never be dirty."

"What about Ray Firebird? Have you smelled him lately?" Ate shouted.

"Would you swing yourself in your hammock?" Ina answered. "Nimo, I'm sorry you heard what the horrible man said about me. He didn't know anything else about me, only that I'm an Indian because of the way I look. He didn't know I'm an assistant manager at Sioux Nation, he didn't know I'm a mother, one of the best cooks on Pine Ridge, a jewelry maker--"

"And the hottest wife in the whole world!" Ate said. Ina rolled her eyes.

"Well, he's right," she said. "My point is people like, what was his name again, Tom, don't know anything about us. They only see our outside, not our inside. That's the real tragedy.

Keep being a nice person, hoksila. Being nice will only make you a better person to other people. Right, Jay Eagle?"

"For the Creator's sake, Josie, I'm always nice!" he shouted. Ina giggled. She gave me a quick hug. Ate came back inside, rubbing his stomach.

"Let's have dinner before I start eating the grass in the yard," Ate said. "By the way, Nimo, since your ina interrupted me earlier, that man is the biggest motherf--"

"Jay Eagle!" Ina said and tugged his ponytail.

It turned out Ate was right about the case being dismissed. He went to court and Tom started calling him a dirty Indian there too, so the nice judge tossed out the battery charge and told Tom to get lost. I was surprised Ate didn't beat Tom a second time.

"I'm sorry Ate," I said. "He shouldn't have said something like that to you."

"Nimo, like I've been trying to tell you, that man is the biggest moth--"

"Jay Eagle," Ina said with a sigh. "We know he's a moth."

In the night, Ate and Ina watched an old movie on TV. They snuggled together under a blanket on the couch. About an hour into the movie, Ate fell asleep.

"Do you want me to carry him to your bed?" I asked Ina.

"Nimo, if you lift him up, you'll die," she said while rubbing her wedding ring. Ina adjusted the blanket over Ate and he snored loudly. Ina groaned. I told Ina goodnight and went to my room, but I remembered I left a toaster pastry in the kitchen. As I passed through the living room, I saw Ina give Ate a kiss on his forehead.

"Goodnight," she told him. "Bonehead."

The Dance

"Geez Nimo, quit holding up the line," John David told me at lunch. "Every time you look at a girl, you stop moving."

"She's so cute," I said and grabbed a slice of pizza from the counter. Michelle Iron Horse had almond shaped eyes with lashes that looked like they were pointing at me. We had health class together at Red Cloud High School. Every time Mr. Perkins talked about 'in-tim-acy,' I looked at Michelle and winked.

"She's an idiot, she's in my art class and she doesn't know the difference between a pen and a pencil," John David said as we walked to our table. "Watch, once we get to 10th grade, she's gonna drop out."

"But she could get her GED," I said.

"Nimo, the only thing she's smart enough to get is an STD," John David said. "Besides, I thought you liked Cindy."

"I do, but she's in California, I can't go to the dance with her."

"Then what's the point of liking her?" John David asked. "That would be like eating burgers when your favorite food is hot dogs."

"But Michelle's still really pretty," I said. "I wonder if she would like to go to the Fall Dance with me."

"Why don't you go over there and tell her you like her instead of staring at her like you're some kind of creep?" John David said when we were at our usual table. We sat at 'Geek Zone,' the table with all the kids in advanced classes. Kids from the other tables usually threw food at us, especially the one Michelle sat at, which John David called 'Dumbass Domination.'

"She'd totally freak out," I said. "Why don't you ask Claudia if she'll go to the dance with me? She still likes you."

"She's going with Scott," he said. "I told her dancing is against my religion. Maybe Michelle does like you, can't hurt to ask. And, you'd quit holding up the line."

"I don't know, I'm too shy," I said. "You do it for me."

"Me?"

"Yeah, all the girls like you. Michelle will listen to you, not me."

"Fine, but you owe me a Big Bat's hot dog for this," he said. John David got up and walked over to Dumbass Domination. He whispered into Michelle's ear and then she looked right at me and said, "You're fat!" loud enough for the whole cafeteria to hear. Most of the other kids pointed at me. They all laughed.

"Oh yeah?" I said and stood on the table so everyone could see me. "Well, I can lose weight and not be fat! You're a bitch and you can't lose that!"

Thanks to my big mouth, I got myself and John David Saturday morning detention. Principal Henderson wanted to suspend us for a week, but my parents and Miss Running Bear came to our rescue by having a meeting with him.

"We can't have Geronimo cussing at other students," Principal Henderson told my parents. "Where could a nice boy like Geronimo learn how to curse like a sailor?" Ina rolled her eyes at Ate. He winked at me.

"Geronimo is a straight A student, he should know better. The same goes for John David. Both of these boys are very intelligent, I just can't understand what made them act so carelessly," Principal Henderson said.

"Nimo does know better, if he was stupid, he wouldn't have called Michelle Iron Horse a bitch in the first place," Ate said.

"Jay Eagle, stop being ridiculous. Nimo, that wasn't a nice thing to say," Ina said. She leaned over to me and whispered, "Not that I'm proud of you or anything, but that's what she gets for calling my hoksila fat."

"I didn't even do anything, I was only the messenger," John David said. "She's the one who called Nimo fat."

"That's true, Mr. Henderson," Miss Running Bear agreed. "If Nimo and John David are going to be penalized, then she should be penalized as well for what she told Nimo. But, my son wasn't doing anything bad except helping out his friend. Don't you remember when you were young and you had your eyes on a girl?"

"Yes," Mr. Henderson admitted. "Okay, Thunderclap and Gutierrez, let's be good gentlemen from now on." John David and me nodded.

"One more slip and both of you won't be going to the Fall Dance," he said.

"Wow, no fall dance?" Ate said. "What's next? No going to the pow wow? There's lots of dancing there, but no, no, no, we can't have these hoksilas dancing around." Ina covered her mouth to giggle. Principal Henderson grunted.

"Can you believe it? He wants to ban us from the dance!" John David said during our bike ride home. "If he bans us, I'm still gonna go and I'll pour punch on him like in that horror movie with the weird girl."

"He said if we slip up again and we won't," I said. "I wanna see if I can take Emily Jumping Bull."

"Nimo, what is it with you and girls?" John David asked. "All the girls at our school look like they got kicked in the face by Bigfoot."

"Aw c'mon, I bet there's a couple girls you like," I said, but I really didn't know. John David never talked to me about his crushes. Even friends I wasn't that close to would tell me who they had their eyes on. I started noticing girls in 4th grade and I couldn't understand why John David hadn't by now.

"No," he said. "There aren't."

"I hear girls talk about you all the time, you must like at least one of them."

"Nope," he said. "I don't."

After dinner, I went to the porch to talk to Ate about John David not being interested in girls. He was carving a beaver figure and when I told him about John David, he didn't seem too surprised.

"Son, have you seen the girls who go to your school?" Ate said.

"Ate," I said. "None of them are as pretty as Cindy, but they're not ugly either. Ina went to my school and you don't think she's ugly, right?"

"Nimo, your ina is so hot that if the stove ever quit working, we could throw the raw food on her face," he said as he smoothed the beaver's tail. "Anyway, don't worry about JD. He'll probably get into girls later. You, my hoksila, need to worry about controlling those teepees you keep building in your pants."

"You mean other people can see them?" I said and darted my

eyes down.

"It's no big deal," Ate said. "Just think about Ray Firebird naked whenever it happens and it'll go away in no time."

"Geez," I said, queasy. "Uh, one more question, Ate. How do you know if a girl is good for you?"

"First thing you gotta do," he said. "Is turn her around and read her nutrition label. A good woman's got a ton of calcium, Vitamin C, zinc, and protein. In fact, your ina has 57 grams of protein, more than average, that's why I married her. Can't have a wife without protein or you'll starve to death."

"Ate, I'm going back inside," I said and stood up.

"Read your ina's nutrition label and you'll see what I'm talking about!"

The week before the Fall Dance, I tried to get a date. I asked Emily Jumping Bull first but she already had one. When I asked who it was, she said, blushing, "I'm going with John David Gutierrez." I figured Emily thought John David was handsome, like every girl at school did. And whenever he spoke Spanish, he spoke it with an accent the girls loved. John David had been teaching me Spanish for a while, but I hadn't mastered the accent just yet. Even if I learned to speak it well, I still wasn't as good looking as him.

I found John David at his locker in between classes. I slammed my hand on his locker and confronted him about asking Emily out when he knew I wanted to do it first.

"I'm not going with her," he said.

"Why would she say that then?" I asked and waved my fist in his face.

"Because she's a lying sack of crap," John David said. "I'm going to the dance, but I'm not going with her or any other girl who's asked me to it."

"Do you wanna double date then?" I said.

"No, I don't wanna double date, I don't even wanna single date."

"How many girls asked you to the dance?"

"Like 30 or 40, maybe more," he said with a shrug. "But I said no."

"You turned them all down?" I gasped. "All of them?!"

"I can dance by myself, Nimo, people do it all the time," he told me, but I found everything a little suspicious. We were freshmen in high school and I was still the only one who thought about making out with girls 24/7. I didn't know if John David was a late bloomer or if I was a horny asshole.

"Try Greta Blue Feather," he said as we walked to math class. "Guys think she's too nerdy, I bet nobody's asked her to the dance yet."

At lunchtime, I sat down next to Greta. I told her she was so pretty, I wished her face was on Mount Rushmore instead of the presidents. But she laughed at me.

"Seriously Nimo?" she said. "Are you sure you can dance without running out of breath?" I was about to do a repeat of the Michelle Iron Horse incident, but I really wanted to go to the Fall Dance with a date. I thought if I couldn't get at least one girl to like me in high school, I was doomed for the rest of my life.

"Face it, Nimo, your date is JD," Greta said and I rolled my eyes. Girls hated me and John David hated girls. I figured we might as well go with each other.

"Are you gonna take me out to dinner first, dance date?" John David asked me with a big smile. I sighed and went to ask Janet Two Bulls at the table across from us. She said I was too fat for her taste. Then I asked her best friend, Hannah Tatanka. She almost fell off her seat from laughing.

"All right, I give up," I said when I sat back down next to John David.

"Me too," he said. "Not worth all the trouble."

"What are you talking about? You can have any girl in this cafeteria," I said. "You can have any girl in this whole school! You can have any girl on the whole rez! If my ina were younger, I bet she would go out with you too!"

"So what?" he shrugged. "I'm good going to the dance by myself."

On the night of the Fall Dance, Ate and Ina dropped me off at the Red Cloud High School gym. Before I went inside, Ina stopped me so she could take a billion pictures of me wearing my best suit.

"Just one more for your unci, okay?" Ina said and made me smile for another picture. "You are so cute, Nimo."

"If I'm cute, how come I don't have a date?"

"Be tough, son. When you was born, you didn't even cry, you yawned. That's why Ina and me named you Geronimo," Ate said.

"Geronimo's Apache name was Goyathlay and it means he who yawns, but we thought Geronimo sounded better," Ina said.

"Ate, Ina, you've told me this story a billion times," I said. "Can I go now?"

"Take care, Nimo," Ate said and patted me on my back. "If you wanna leave early, call me and I'll come get you."

"Ask some girls to dance with you, Nimo. I'm sure they'll say yes," Ina said.

"They'll probably ask me where John David is so they can dance with him instead," I muttered to myself.

When I went inside the gym, I saw John David by the punch bowl. He was staring hard at the ladle. I asked him if something was up.

"Yeah," he said. "Something's really wrong. I'm not sure I can talk about it."

"I'm your best friend, you can tell me anything. So what is it?"

"I'll tell you later, after the dance is over."

For most of the dance, we stood by the punch bowl, talking smack about everyone who passed by us. Claudia and Scott were on the dancefloor. Claudia winked at John David. He groaned and looked away.

"Jealous, JD?" Scott said. "What about you, Nimo? Couldn't even get a ghost to dance with you, huh?"

"Stuff it, toilet paper," John David said. Scott reached out for John David's neck, but I stepped between them. Claudia was stuck up and Scott was a jerk – they were made for each other.

Soon enough, it was the end of the night and prizes were about to be given out. Claudia and Scott won best dancers and Greta and her date, Joshua Redshirt, won best dressed couple. Principal Henderson announced there was one prize left.

"Cutest couple that should be together but aren't, at least, not yet," Mr. Henderson said on the gym stage. "John David Gutierrez and Emily Jumping Bull!" John David was grabbed by a crowd of people and dragged onto the stage. I clapped for him, but he didn't seem happy. He turned his head from side to side, like he was looking for an escape.

"Help me," he mouthed in Spanish, but I didn't know what to do.

"Give Emily a kiss on the cheek, John David. She's gorgeous, don't you think so?" Principal Henderson said. He handed the microphone to John David and he answered with one word: No. Everyone in the gym gasped and booed him. Principal Henderson said he'd get Saturday detention for a month if he didn't apologize to Emily.

"I don't think she's ugly," John David said, but it didn't help much since Emily was in tears. "It's just, I don't think she's pretty."

"Gutierrez, you say you're sorry this instant," Principal Henderson said. "I don't know what's gotten into you, young man." John David looked at me and I saw a tear slide down his right cheek.

"What's wrong, JD?" Scott said through all the jeering. "Don't like girls?" John David took the microphone from Principal Henderson and cleared his throat.

"All right, you all really wanna know why I don't think she's pretty? I'm gay, dammit! I like boys!" John David shouted. Everyone erupted in laughs, but when John David didn't say anything else, they went back to booing him. They called him gross, pervert, sissy, and words I don't want to think about. Even Principal Henderson joined in and called John David a waste of a handsome young man. I grabbed the punch bowl, ran up to the stage, and poured what was left on Principal Henderson.

"Thunderclap! Gutierrez! Get over here now!" Principal Henderson yelled with the bowl still on his head. John David and me ran out of the gym and we didn't stop running until we got to Big Bat's.

"I'll call my ate to come get us," I panted. "Man, I thought we were gonna get beat up. C'mon, let's go inside for some grub."

"Wait, wait, wait," John David said and pulled my arm. "Are we still friends?"

"Yeah, why wouldn't we be?"

"But, Nimo, I'm gay," he said.

"I know, I heard you." We sat on the sidewalk, next to a couple of hungry dogs.

"I thought you wouldn't wanna, you know, be my friend anymore," he said. "I figured you'd think I'm gross or something."

"Why would I?" I said. "You're gay, you're not Ray Firebird." John David scratched his head. He opened his mouth to talk more, but tears came out of his eyes. He pulled his shirt over his face.

"John David?" I said, surprised. He never cried about anything. When we were in fourth grade, we both fell off a tall slide during recess. I hit my elbow so hard, I couldn't help but cry. John David slammed down on his knees and they bruised and bled right then. He stood up and said, "That was awesome! I'm gonna do it again."

"I don't wanna quit being friends with you, Nimo," he said through his sniffles. "Really. You're my best friend." I scooted myself closer to him.

"We promised to be best friends forever back in third grade, remember?"

"Are you okay with me being gay?" he asked. "If you're not, that's fine."

"Lots of people are gay. A lot of writers I like are gay. Oscar Wilde was gay, David Sedaris is gay, Elizabeth Bishop was gay, Langston Hughes was gay and so was Tennessee Williams. Remember when we read his play The Glass Menagerie in English class last year? It's no big deal." He frowned a little.

"Some people do think it's a big deal, Nimo," he said. "Like

Principal Henderson and everyone else who booed me tonight. Especially Scott."

"Well they're stupid," I said and stood up. "Scott is nothing but a big roll of toilet paper anyway. Who cares what he thinks? People wipe their butts with him." John David laughed, finally.

"Buddies?" I said and put my pinky close to his hands. We did our usual pinky swear. We walked inside Big Bat's to get some food. John David lowered himself to my ear. He whispered, "Thanks Nimo."

"No problem," I said. "Now let's eat, I'm starving."

The Funeral

wo salesmen from Edison Electricity rang the doorbell at 6 in the morning. Ate answered and told the men we weren't interested. They begged him to switch to their company, so Ate said we were Amish and slammed the door in their faces.

"Ate, can you drive me to school? One of my bikes tires popped," I said when he got back to the breakfast table.

"Sorry son," he said. "I gotta hustle, I'm redoing all the floors at work today."

"I'll take you, Nimo," Ina said. "Finish your scrambled eggs."

"I don't like eggs, they come out of the chicken's butt," I said.

"Nimo, I don't like you 'cause you came outta Ina," Ate said.

"He didn't come out of my butt!" Ina said. She pulled on his ponytail and got back to eating the last of her breakfast. I took in a small mouthful of my eggs and washed it all down with my chocolate milk. When Ate got up to get more coffee, the phone rang.

"For the Creator's sake, I hope it ain't salesmen again," he said and picked up. "What the hell do you want this early, you little twerp? Yeah, I'm Josephine Thunderclap's husband, what the hell do you want from us? Who? Oh."

"What's going on, honey?" Ina asked. Ate thanked the person for calling and hung up. He put his hand over his face for a minute before he spoke.

"It was about your ina, Josie," he said. "She died in her sleep, baby."

Government stats say life expectancy for a Lakota woman on Pine Ridge rez is about 50. Unci was 63, so she beat the average age. She was born in 1939 near the Wounded Knee massacre site. She married my tunkasila, John David Red Cloud, when she was 23 and had to Ina not long after. Tunkasila John David was the chief of Pine Ridge and an EMT, two stressful jobs at once. Unci Sequoia had her own jewelry business. They used most of their money on booze. Ina once told me Unci drank ten beers a day, but quit after I was born. It didn't seem like it helped her. A heart attack took her while she slept. Her mailman thought something was up when she didn't answer her door. She always got on his case because she liked privacy and she couldn't stand how he knew her address. When she didn't come out to insult him, he called an ambulance and the paramedics found her.

"I'm sorry about your granny," John David told me at school during lunch. "If you need to stay home, I'll pick up your homework for you."

"I'll be okay," I said. "We're burying her at the cemetery across the street so I might as well keep coming to school." Though I loved Red Cloud High School, I hated seeing Red Cloud Cemetery every day. Chief Red Cloud, my really great tunkasila, is buried there, and tourists love taking pictures next to his grave like he's a landmark.

When I got home from school, there were about thirty people standing in front of my house with baskets of food. I opened the door and they all came in, set their food down, and gave me words of respect. Even Scott Black Bear showed up with baskets of bread his parents baked for us.

"Hope you like it, Nimo," Scott said. "Later today, I'll be back with Claudia. She and Mrs. Graywolf are making you some special hot dogs."

"Thanks Scott," I said and took the baskets from his huge hands. "I didn't think you'd come by."

"Hey, your unci was a chief's wife," he said. "I may not like you very much, but I gotta respect the dead, especially the widow of a chief. See you, fatso."

"Tell your parents I said thanks, toilet paper."

"Tell John David he's a fruit," he said. "A big, giant fruit."

When I thought everyone left, Mrs. Yellow Fire came over. She handed me a giant plate of her famous extra fudge brownies.

"You tell your parents I came by, okay?" she said. "If you want any extra brownies, let me know." I nodded and she patted me on the back. Her husband, Eddie Yellow Fire, died of a drug overdose in 2000. Ate built Eddie's coffin so Mrs. Yellow Fire wouldn't have to buy one.

My parents came home from work late. They had each taken an overtime shift to pay for the funeral. Ina took a bite of one of Mrs. Yellow Fire's brownies, but didn't finish it. She wrapped it in a napkin and told me and Ate goodnight. I sat on the couch with Ate, watching Roseanne, and eating a bowl of Miss Running Bear's fruit salad.

"Isn't this the one where Roseanne's dad dies?" I asked. Ate nodded.

"Yeah, I love this episode. Listen, son, if you don't wanna go to school tomorrow, you don't have to. I'm taking time off and Ina ain't gonna work for a while."

"Why are you taking time off? I thought you hated Unci," I said.

"She hated me," he said. "Honestly, she was one of the worst people I ever knew. She was despicable, spiteful, and only cared about herself. But hell, Nimo, that evil, disgusting, buck toothed, Loch Ness monster, Bigfoot looking woman gave birth to the woman I love. She might have hated me with all her heart, but without her, I wouldn't be married to the best, sweetest, most beautiful woman I've ever known. I can't ever hate her, son, not even if I tried. Something so good in my life came from something so bad."

The next morning, I went to Principal Eagle Bull's office and gave her a note from my parents. She didn't even read it – she just told me I could come back whenever I was 'done grieving.' Principal Eagle Bull took over Principal Henderson after he retired and she was much nicer than him.

"When's the funeral, Thunderclap?" Principal Eagle Bull asked.

"Saturday at two," I said. "At the tribal office."

"Thank you, Thunderclap," she said. "I'll make an announcement this afternoon. Your unci was a fine woman. You must be proud to be her grandson."

At lunch, I found John David at the vending machine. A bag of chips he bought got stuck and he kicked the machine twice. I reached in my pocket, found spare change, and got him another bag, but they were barbecue chips.

"Barbecue? Gross!" he said and handed the bag to me. "Hey, I thought you weren't coming to school today."

"I wasn't, but I can't stand being home," I said and munched on some of the barbecue chips. "Everyone keeps coming over, dropping food off, and crying."

"Yeah, my grandpa on my dad's side croaked when I was six," John David said. "All of my family from Costa Rica came to Brooklyn and man, were they annoying. I faked a fever so I wouldn't have to leave my room."

"I'm not coming to school tomorrow and Friday," I said. "I wish funerals weren't complicated. You know what, John David? If I die before you do, just throw me in the trash and call it a day."

"I'll give you the fanciest trash bag there is," he said. "If I die first, toss me in a lake and let a swamp monster take care of me."

"Then it's a deal," I said and we pinky swore.

Principal Eagle Bull made the announcement about Unci's funeral when I was in my history class and Ms. Plenty Wounds said I could go home. I tried to tell her I didn't want to, but she was already making a speech to the class about how great my unci was, especially because she was the wife of a chief. I went to my locker, grabbed all my stuff, and headed to my bike outside of the school. Before going home, I pedaled to Red Cloud Cemetery and stopped at my really great tunkasila's headstone. People were gathered around it, posing by it and smiling for their cameras.

On Thursday morning, a salesman from Super Sonic Hearing Aids rang the doorbell and told Ate 75% of Lakota people suffer from severe hearing loss.

"What? Sorry, I can't hear you!" Ate said and slammed the door shut. Ate's new temporary job was answering the phone and the door. He seemed relieved it was a salesman and not another person's famous recipe.

"We got news for you, Nimo," Ina told me as I poured syrup over my stack of pancakes. "Unci put you in her will."

"That's right, son, a whole five dollars," Ate said and Ina pulled on his ponytail.

"You're getting $2,000 for college," Ina went on. "And her old car. But, there's one thing you gotta do. She chose you to write her eulogy."

"Aw Ina, I can't do that," I said. "I don't even know how to write a check."

"That ain't true," Ina said. "Remember when you was in 7th grade and you wrote a short story and won 50 bucks? You'll think of something. Your unci loved all your poems and all your stories. Look what she wrote in her will, hoksila. 'Geronimo is going to be a famous writer someday. I might not live to see it, but I know it will happen.'"

"Ina, I can't write a eulogy," I said. "What am I gonna say?"

"Oh Nimo, for the Creator's sake," she said. "She was your unci – you knew her better than most people on the rez. Just write whatever comes to your head."

In the afternoon, I helped Ate rake leaves on the lawn. After we were done, I sat with him on the porch, and he told me about the first time he met Unci. He said it was on June 9, 1983 – his first date with Ina.

"I had a bag of nuts with me. I ate some of them in the kitchen while I waited for Ina to get ready. Your unci said to me, Jay Eagle Thunderclap, you touch my daughter and I'll take your nuts. So I said, Mrs. Red Cloud, you can have these,

83

I got another bag in my car." We laughed together. I wished Unci would have thought Ate was funny.

"Ate," I said. "I feel really bad, but I haven't cried for her yet. She wasn't very nice to me, you, or pretty much anyone. This sounds mean, but I don't think I miss her."

"Don't feel too bad about it, not like anyone's actually gonna miss her, except for your ina and stray dogs she fed. I am gonna miss heckling her though, that was always fun."

"Was she really that bad, Ate? You knew her longer than I did. What was she like?"

"Honestly, she was a horrible woman, but she wasn't the worst woman in the world either. You see, Nimo, there are two types of people in the world. There are people who are messed up, but they got a good heart. There are people who ain't messed up, but they ain't got a good heart. Your unci was the first type."

John David and Miss Running Bear came over for dinner. They brought roast chicken, garlic bread, and macaroni and cheese. It was enough food to last for a couple of days and our refrigerator was already packed. Most people on Pine Ridge are poor and I never forgot what it was like to be poor. There were times when I'd take a bath with cold water because we couldn't pay the gas and times when I wouldn't take a bath at all because we couldn't pay the water. Yet whenever someone died, food was suddenly everywhere, even at the funeral itself. Back when we didn't have much to eat, as terrible as it sounds, we waited for somebody to die.

"You get to make the eulogy?" John David said while we sat on the porch after dinner. "That's awesome, I bet it's gonna be really good."

"No it's not," I said. "I don't know why she picked me. What if I screw up?"

"What are you talking about? You've written like a thousand stories and poems, right? How is a eulogy any different? It's a story of someone's life."

"But what if it sucks?"

"Geez Nimo! It's not like she's gonna come out of her coffin and strangle you if it sucks, she's dead!" John David said and I laughed. I knew he was right.

The day before Unci's funeral, I rode my bike to her house in Wounded Knee. I thought I could get some inspiration for her eulogy by visiting the place where she died. It took me about two hours to get there because people kept stopping me on the road to talk about Unci. They seemed to be more torn up about her death than I was.

Unci's house stood on a raised piece of land, no neighbors close by, just the way she preferred to live. Her car was parked diagonally across her lawn. The Pine Ridge flag hanging from her porch post was about to fall over, so I adjusted it before it could hit the ground. I had a key to Unci's house. She gave it to me for my 12th birthday. When I asked her about it, she told me, "Takoja, one day I'm gonna croak and someone needs to get my corpse out before it stinks up my house."

Everything inside looked the same as usual. There were cups on the kitchen counter with coffee residue on the bottom and plates with stale bread crusts on them. I walked to the living room and saw the large portrait of my grandparents on their wedding day in 1962. They were holding hands and smiling. I loved that picture of them because it was proof they had been happy with each other, even if it was only for a moment. Ina told me their marriage was rocky and they fought almost every day, but sometimes she'd catch them in the middle of a hug or a kiss. Unci's rocking chair leaned to one side with a small piece of paper underneath it. I picked it up to read what it said: Remember to ask Josie if her blockhead husband can fix this.

Before I left, I went to Unci's bedroom. As much as I visited her house when I was little, she never let me go to her room. She told me I could only go in her room when I turned 37. I swung the door open and saw an old, ripped mattress on the floor and an empty bottle of liquor. There was a picture frame on the floor turned face down and I assumed it was of Tunkasila John David or Ina. But it was a picture of me as a newborn.

As I pedaled back home, Ate and Ina drove past me. They waited for me to catch up. When I got to them, they asked if I finished writing the eulogy. I told them no.

"Nimo, the funeral's tomorrow, you gotta say something," Ate said.

"Load your bike in the truck, we'll drive you home," Ina said. I put my bike up and got in the backseat. They were upset I hadn't written anything and I agreed with them. Unci wasn't a huge part of my life, but she was the only grandparent I had in my life. Not being able to talk about her made me look like a total jerk.

"Ina, what are some nice things Unci did when she was alive? Did she do anything nice for you or for my tunkasila?"

"Well," Ina began, slowly. "Once, when I was a little younger than you, there was a hoksila at school who called me ugly. She showed up at the school with some hot water and almost poured it on him. For your tunkasila, there was a time when he bought her some flowers and she said, 'Oh, look at this here. Wasted money.'"

The Funeral

"That doesn't sound nice, Ina."

"No, I guess it don't," she said. "Good luck with the eulogy, hoksila."

In the night, I sat on the porch with a notepad, scribbling details about Unci. Everything I wrote was either not important or not nice.

Hi everyone, my name is Geronimo Jay Thunderclap and my unci was an alcoholic who didn't have a bed. She also hated everybody. I'm sure she hated everyone in this room. Please leave all food with my parents. If you brought anything sweet, please give it to me. Thanks for stopping by! Now let's start digging the hole!

"Son, you're still up?" Ate said when he stepped out on the porch with a glass of water in his hand. "It's one in the morning."

"I'm trying to come up with something decent," I said. "Is Ina still awake?"

"No, she knocked right out but she kept kicking me, so I'm up now. You ready for your big moment tomorrow?"

"I got nothing," I admitted. "I'll go up there and say whatever. I wish Unci told me she picked me before she died."

"Son, you can't prepare for things like this," Ate said. "This afternoon, me and Ina went to the funeral home and the people there were talking at 100 miles an hour. Ina threw her hands up and told them, 'forget it, I'll bury her in my backyard.'"

"How did you deal with funerals when your ate and ina died?" I asked him.

"When my ina died, I was six. I didn't understand what happened. I thought she went on a trip and she'd be back eventually," he said. "My ate died when I was 16. We buried him two days after and I had a dream with him on the same day.

He said, dammit hoksila, I'm stuck in eternity with relatives I hate, you and your ciye get my shovel and unbury me right now." I laughed and Ate gave me a one-armed hug.

"What were they like, Ate?" I asked. "You don't talk about them that much."

"I can't say much about my ina," he said and took a seat on the porch chair next to me. "I've heard about her from some of my relatives. My unci and tunkasila, her ina and ate, talked about her tons. They missed her every single day. I've heard she was funny, she was pretty, she was sweet, but I barely remember anything."

"Do you remember her being alive?"

"Kinda," he said, sipping on his water. "I remember her singing an old Lakota lullaby to me whenever I couldn't sleep, the one me and Ina used to sing to you. Other than that, I don't remember much. As for my ate, he was hilarious, one of the funniest guys ever, but not as funny as my tunkasila James Eagle. Your tunkasila Frank Thunderclap was also a big drinker though. He might have been funny, but when he was drunk, he was mean."

"How mean?" I asked.

"Nimo, he was so mean, he used to beat me and your leksi all the time," he said, looking down at his slippers. "Over dumb stuff, too. Once he punched me in my gut for not washing his favorite mug. Why didn't I wash it? He smashed the damn thing against the wall while he was drunk and didn't even remember doing that. He punched me so hard, I threw up on the floor and then he hit me again for getting some of my puke on his rug. I was 12 when that happened, Nimo. I swore I would never, ever be the kind of ate he was to me. I'm not perfect, but hell, I ain't ever tasted alcohol, not after what it did to my ate and lots of our relatives."

I looked over at Ate and he gulped down the rest of his water. Part of his belly popped out from underneath his Black Sabbath t-shirt. I knew my tunkasila Frank used to beat him up, but I never knew just how bad it was. After Tunkasila Frank died, Ate and Leksi Gray Mountain got jobs in Sioux Plains and worked to take care of themselves. Leksi even went to college while working three part time jobs. Ate sometimes worked two full time jobs or four part time ones. He tried getting his GED, but he said school and work was too much for him. Ina's life wasn't that much better either. She once told me she wished she at least had a sibling like Ate because whenever her parents were fighting or drunk or spending days at a bar off the rez, she had no one to talk to. I didn't know how my parents survived their younger days, but they did. People always tell me, "Nimo, you come from strong ancestors" because I have chiefs in my family tree. But I think everyone who's alive today comes from strong ancestors. Everyone alive right now is here because their ancestors survived whatever faced them.

"Hey Ate," I said. "When your time comes, where do you wanna be buried?"

"Aw Nimo," Ate sighed and stretched his arms up towards the sky. "When I die, just do me one favor – miss me."

The tribal office was packed with people by the time I got there with my parents. There was a banner over the door that said "Rest in Peace, Mrs. Sequoia Red Cloud." I couldn't look at it for too long because I knew Ate's and Ina's names would be on a banner someday. Since so many people showed up, some watched the funeral from outside through the windows. My parents, John David, and Miss Running Bear sat in the front row. Leksi Gray Mountain, Tunwinla Rosa, and Lucille were in the second row. I don't know exactly how many people came to Unci's funeral, but I'd guess the number was somewhere in the thousands. There were several tables against the walls of the room, all of them packed with food. Behind the podium was the portrait of Unci and Tunkasila on their wedding day. After everyone settled down, I stepped to the podium.

"Uh, hi," I said into the microphone. "I'm Geronimo Jay Thunderclap, which all of you already know. I'm Sequoia Red Cloud's grandson. She was married to Chief John David Red Cloud, which all of you know too and I don't know why I'm still talking."

"Nimo, you're doing great," Ina whispered to me. "I love you." I pulled out my eulogy from my pocket. I wrote it while I ate breakfast earlier that day. It was crumpled and some of the ink rubbed off. I thought back to the episode of All in the Family when Archie needed to write a eulogy for his best friend, Stretch Cunningham. If Archie Bunker could do a eulogy, I figured I could too if I tried hard enough.

"My unci was a private person. Some of you probably saw her house, the one up on the hilly road in Wounded Knee. She hated other people knowing her address. She didn't even like the mailman because he knew where she lived," I went on and to my surprise, everyone laughed a little.

"But as much as she hated being around people, she accepted everybody, no matter what. When John David Gutierrez came out, she told him, 'JD, if you want a cute guy to hook up with, I got a really cute takoja named Nimo,'" I said. Everyone laughed louder this time.

"Of course, my unci wasn't all good. She was a drunk and talked about everyone behind their backs. In fact, sometimes

I wished she wasn't my unci at all. Most days, I thought she didn't like me. And, everybody thinks she hated my ate, but that's not true. A couple years ago, she told me 'your ate's a good man, but don't ever tell him I said that because then he'll talk to me.' My unci was an expert at giving off a tough appearance. She could have probably taken down Mount Rushmore with her bare hands. I might not have felt like a prized grandson a lot, but I know she loved me, in her own weird way. I know for sure she loved Pine Ridge and she loved all of us, even if she never said it. She loved my ina. I know this because she would call every day and ask my ina the same question – 'has Jay Eagle screwed up?' She only asked this because she cared about my ina. My unci had her problems, like everybody, but that didn't make her a bad person. Problems made her human. There are two types of people in the world. The first type are people who are messed up, but they got a good heart. The second type are people who ain't messed up, but they ain't got a good heart. My unci was the first type."

I looked up and saw tears pouring down Ina's cheeks. I got down from the podium and walked to Unci's open coffin as the drummers, including Ate and Leksi, started singing a memorial song for her. Sometimes when Unci would watch me when I was little, she'd fall asleep in her rocking chair with her long, gray hair dangling on her left side. The only difference now was she wasn't in her rocking chair.

I biked to school early on Monday morning so I could stop by Red Cloud Cemetery to say hello to my ancestors. Years ago, when I first visited Rosebud, Ate's home rez, he showed me the Thunderclap family plots at Blue Water Creek Cemetery.

Tunkasila Frank Thunderclap had a fatal heart attack in 1978. Before him, Kunsi Lucille Thunderclap committed suicide by overdosing on sleeping pills in 1968. Tunkasila John David died in 1989 of kidney failure. Nellie died before she was even born. Lakota people usually have big families and I do too – most of mine just happens to be dead.

I finally walked over to Unci's fresh grave. She had a wooden marker with SEQUOIA RED CLOUD 1939-2002 carved into it. Ate made it for her until her concrete tombstone was ready.

"Hey Unci," I said. "I hope Tunkasila JD is keeping you company. I brought something for you." I reached into my pocket and put her house key underneath the marker. Then I got on my bike, said toksa to my relatives, and went to find John David at the front of the school.

The Cigarette

*M*y parents were always known as the cutest couple on Pine Ridge rez. Whenever they argued, I thought "this is the divorce fight." Once, they didn't talk at all because Ate forgot to pay the phone bill.

"We gotta pay a $30 fee to get the phone back on, you idiot," Ina said.

"We are Lakota! We don't need a phone, we got smoke signals!" Ate said and Ina didn't talk for him for a whole day. They made up after Ate came home with a receipt from the phone company. He folded it into a flower and wrote SORRY in blue ink.

But that fight definitely wasn't in the divorce category. I started working with Ate and Mr. Black Bear at Spotted Elk College a few weeks after the phone bill fight as an assistant handyman, or as Ate would say a 'facility technician.' Since I was in school and playing football, Ate only scheduled me for ten hours a week. For the first few days, Ate watched my every move to make sure I wasn't goofing off.

"You can go home now, Nimo," he said on my fifth day of

work.

"But you're supposed to show me how to fix a flickering light."

"Don't you got homework?" he asked and I sighed. He told me he'd clock me out and then he walked outside towards the dumpsters.

I was in my car when I realized I left my backpack in the workroom. Ate still hadn't made me a key yet, so I drove around to the dumpster area to find him. I saw him standing against the brick wall with his blue shades on, shirt sleeves rolled up, and a cigarette in his mouth.

"Sons of bitches!" Ate said when he saw me. He threw his cigarette in the air.

"Sorry," I said. "I forgot my backpack in the workroom."

"Well then go get it, don't come over here and give me a heart attack."

"Ate, I don't have a key yet," I reminded him.

"Go find Mr. Black Bear and tell him to let you inside."

"He's out sick today, remember?" I said. Ate cursed loudly. He told me to wait in my car while he went to get my backpack for me. When he returned, he was mumbling to himself, probably more curse words.

"Why are you doing it, Ate?" I asked him as he handed me my backpack. "You already quit smoking twice before."

"I'm getting fat," he said and grabbed his stomach. "I don't get hungry when I smoke." Over the years, my whole family put on weight. Ina was the only one who didn't get too fat, just stockier than before. Once Ate and Ina got better jobs, they bought all kinds of food, but it was mostly junk.

"Don't tell Ina," Ate said as he adjusted his ponytail. "I'll quit right when I drop a couple pounds, I promise." His tattoos were shiny since he was sweating so much. His left arm has Ina's name in script letters and his right arm has mine and Nellie's in the same letters. Ate waved at me and I took off towards home.

On Friday, I went to Big Bat's with John David after school. Claudia and Scott were there, kissing up a storm in the booth next to us. Mr. Graywolf came over to them with a spray bottle.

"Cut it out," he said as he sprinkled water on them. "Don't you see Nimo and John David are trying to eat?"

"Everyone knows how much John David loves hot dogs," Scott said. Mr. Graywolf sprayed him right in the face.

"I don't allow hate talk in my business," Mr. Graywolf said. "You better watch it, hoksila. Nimo's father is your father's boss." Everyone else inside Big Bat's chanted "Tell him, Wayne Graywolf, tell him!"

"I'll call you later," Scott said to Claudia. He pointed to me and John David. "You know, if you guys keep being friends, everyone's gonna think you're a couple."

"A cuter couple than you and your mom," John David said. He raised a fist at us, but Mr. Graywolf sprayed him in the face again. Scott and Claudia went outside to finish their kissing session.

"My ate took up smoking again," I said to John David.

"So what? Is he not sharing his cigarettes with you?"

"He's got a heart problem, he's not supposed to smoke at all," I said. "On Monday, I saw him smoke two cigarettes and yesterday, I saw him smoke seven."

"Oh, that's bad. Try to talk to him about it."

"Yeah, like he's gonna listen to me. What do you think I

should do?"

"I don't know, maybe spray him with water like Mr. Gray-wolf."

As I drove John David back to his house, he kept on fiddling with the radio. He tuned it to all the different stations until he finally settled for a love song.

"I thought you hated love songs," I said and he told me to shut up.

"You know that guy who just moved here from California? The one in our biology class?" he said.

"Ignacio? Yeah, what about him?"

"He's really cute. And he's really smart too. He always makes hundreds on our quizzes and tests. I'm thinking of asking him out."

"What?" I said. "Him? He's not even gay."

"He might be."

"He doesn't look gay."

"What does gay look like? You think we walk around in glitter covered suits?'"

"That's not what I meant!" I said. "Ignacio doesn't seem gay is what I wanted to say. He's real buff, good at sports, and all the girls love him."

"Wow, Nimo. You just described me."

"Yeah, you're right," I said. "How did you ever know you were gay anyway?"

"I knew forever," he told me. "I wasn't sure at first, but then I was. Me and my ina were watching Gone with the Wind one night. Instead of looking at Vivian Leigh, I was eyeing Clark Gable. The next day, I got my glitter suit in the mail."

"All right, I get your point, John David," I said. We high fived each other when I reached his house.

At dinner that night, Ina swore she smelled smoke. She went to check if the oven was still on and when she sat back down next to Ate, he fell off his chair and hit his head on the floor.

"Jay Eagle, I just mopped the floor!" Ina said. Ina went to the bathroom to get him pain killers. While she was gone, he grabbed his cologne and doused himself with it.

"Ate, she's gonna find out sooner or later," I said, coughing.

"She ain't gonna find out nothing if you shut up," Ate said.

"Jay Eagle, did you really need that much cologne?" Ina said with a few gags when she came back with the pill bottle.

"I just let out the biggest fart of my life," Ate said. "I'm sparing your nose."

"You remember my ate's old saying," Ina said. "You're not ready for marriage until you're comfortable enough to fart in front of each other."

When I went to work on Monday, Ate showed me how to stop leaks. We lied down next to each other under the sink in the faculty bathroom and he taught me how pipes worked. I couldn't listen to him very well. Every time he talked, smoke smell got in my eyes. After my pipe lesson, we went to the faculty lounge to repair some ceiling tiles. Ate brought out his ladder and as he climbed up, his pack of cigarettes fell out of his pocket.

"Ate, when are you gonna quit?" I asked him.

"Why the hell should I quit? I'm the head technician. If I quit, you're gone too."

"No, I mean smoking," I said. Ate told me it was none of my business. When I asked him again before my shift ended, he said if I asked about his smoking one more time, he'd make me work a double shift every Friday night.

"Ate, what about your heart?"

"The hell with my heart, Nimo. It don't even work right in the first place. Listen, either you get back to work or I'll let you go. Mr. Black Bear loves overtime hours."

After my shift was over, I grabbed my stuff and headed to John David's house.

"I tried talking to him, it didn't work," I said. "He threatened to fire me."

"That's bull," John David said. "I bet if you smoked, he'd freak."

"I should smoke a couple of his cigarettes to get back at him," I said.

"You can't smoke, you don't even like candy cigs," John David said. "Hey, I got an idea. How about tomorrow after school, we get some Jägermeister?"

"We can't get booze, we're only 16."

"It's easy, you just get a bottle and go to the cashier who looks the dumbest."

"Hell, I'm in," I said. It sounded like a great idea to me.

Liquor is illegal on Pine Ridge, but that doesn't stop anyone from getting it if they want it. My parents always warned me about drinking since it messed up a bunch of our relatives. Ate once told me that when my tunkasila Frank Thunderclap had his heart attack, he clutched a beer in each hand. Decades ago, my Thunderclap and Red Cloud families were big. They could have stayed big if some of them hadn't let their drinking get out of control.

On Tuesdays, I didn't work, so John David and me got into my car and we took off to get some Jägermeister like he suggested. I was a little uneasy about drinking, but Ate should have been uneasy about smoking.

"Maybe you should do it, Nimo. You look older than me," John David said when we got to Grocery Ed's just outside of Pine Ridge. He pointed down at his Teenage Mutant Ninja Turtles t-shirt and then to my plaid button down shirt.

"But you're older than me."

"Only by five months, just get in there."

"What if this goes over? I don't even have a fake ID."

"Relax Nimo," he said. "Go inside before Ray Firebird shows up and buys the whole freakin' aisle."

"I don't even know what to buy."

"Jägermeister," he said. "Or whatever says alcohol on it."

"Okay, wait here," I gave in. I regretted shaving my tiny mustache earlier in the day. Before I went inside, I straightened my ponytail and tucked my shirt in.

As soon as I walked through the automatic doors, three people from Pine Ridge were in my face. Hi Nimo! How's your ina and ate? How's school going? How's picking out colleges going for you? Have you written any new stories? I answered every question and quickly walked to the back of the store. There was one bottle of Jägermeister left on the shelf. I grabbed the bottle and a package of trail mix for a snack.

"Nimo Thunderclap!" a voice said when I was halfway to the checkout lines. It was my neighbor, Mrs. Yellow Fire. I totally forgot she worked at Grocery Ed's.

"Whatcha got there, Nimo? I can check you out at register four."

"Oh, I, uh, forgot to get something, I guess I'll see you later," I said and took off to a place she'd never find me – the feminine needs aisle. There was a man staring at tampons and hyperventilating. He looked over 21 for sure.

"Hey buddy," I said. "How about I buy those tampons your lady needs and you buy me this booze? I'll even give you this trail mix."

"Are you from Pine Ridge?" he asked.

"Yeah, I'm Lakota. This Jägermeister's for a special ritual going on tonight. Care to help me out?" I said. He swiped the bottle from my hands and told me his name – Will Howard. He was the motivational speaker who made the alcohol prevention presentations at Red Cloud High School. Instead of telling me to get lost like anyone else would have, he gave me a speech about how 'firewater' was ruining the Lakota Sioux tribe. He had a few good points here and there, but his speech was so long, I could have driven to Sioux Plains and back to Grocery Ed's and he'd still be talking.

"I'm calling your parents, kid," Mr. Howard said. "You should've known better."

"I'm sorry," I said. "Let me off this time?" He thought about it for a second and he told me to go home and think about his speech. I thanked him and went to pay for my trail mix. When I was about to drive back to Pine Ridge, my parents pulled up.

"Go home, JD, Nimo's grounded," Ate said.

"I can't, he drove me here," John David shrugged.

As if Mr. Howard's speech wasn't enough, I had to stand in the parking lot listening to my parents yell at me in English and Lakota.

"You know what alcohol did to our family, what the hell are you doing out here trying to buy some?" Ina shouted.

"I am so mad at you right now, Nimo!" Ate said, his face all scrunched up.

"Calm down, Jay Eagle, you have a bad heart," Ina told him.

"Let my heart blow up if it needs to, Josie! I'm angry!" he said.

Ate got out of his truck and ran inside Grocery Ed's while Ina kept on yelling at me.

"Drink this," Ate said when he got back. "You want it so much, here you go." He was holding a bottle, but it wasn't Jägermeister. I drank a few sips. A minute later, I puked. It wasn't until I was emptied out that I realized it was only sparkling cider.

"Geez Nimo, don't be such a lightweight," John David said.

"Have you learned your lesson now, son?" Ate asked.

"What lesson?" I groaned and held my stomach.

"Don't you act like you don't know what we're talking about, Geronimo Jay Thunderclap," Ina said. "You are grounded for a month."

"But Ate's been smoking behind your back for weeks," I blurted. John David looked up at the sky. Ate's eyes twitched.

"Nimo, you get your butt home this instant," Ina said to me. John David jumped into the passenger seat and I started the car. As we drove away from my parents, I heard Ina tell Ate she was going to kill him by shoving cigarettes down his throat.

"That was intense," John David said. "My parents fought just like that right before they split up."

"I don't think they'd split up," I shrugged. "Do you?"

"How should I know?" he said. "They're your parents."

Saturday came and Ate and Ina were still not speaking to each other. Ate spent the morning carving figurines on the porch. Ina sat in the living room, making earrings and necklaces. They ate and slept in different parts of the house. Ate stopped shaving and stubble appeared over his upper lip and on his chin, just the way Ina hated. I asked Ina if I could go hang out with John David even though I was still grounded.

"Sure," she said. "Dinner will be ready at six."

When I got to John David's, Miss Running Bear said he was grounded. I told her everything that happened so she'd ease up on him and she laughed in my face.

"I knew your dad was doing something," Miss Running Bear said. "I saw him buying cigarettes at Big Bat's last week. He told me they were for you."

She let John David come out of his room and we headed to Big Bat's for lunch. While we waited for our food, Ignacio Puente walked inside. His parents were the Pentecostal missionaries who visited Pine Ridge every year to help families out, but now they moved permanently to the rez. He was over six feet tall with a light, black mustache and toned muscles over all his arms and legs.

"Hey guys," he said to John David and me. "Good to see you in here."

"Hi Ignacio," John David said. "If you wanna eat with us, there's always an extra chair waiting for you." I never heard John David be so nice to anyone. He didn't like too much company around him. It was a miracle we even became best friends.

"I'm just here for a small chocolate milkshake," Ignacio said. "I need some fuel before my run. I'll see you two around." He made his way over to the counter to place his order with Mrs. Graywolf.

"He's got a great ass," John David whispered.

"Hey, hey, we're about to eat here," I said.

"I gotta listen to you say how hot you think Cindy Blackbird is all the time, you can listen to me talk about how hot Ignacio is for five seconds," he said.

"What if he's not gay?" I asked. John David didn't answer me.

As Ignacio passed by our table, his eyes stayed still. Ignacio waved to us before he walked out and I heard John David whisper, "The Creator is real."

Ate and Ina reached eight days without speaking. I went to work on Wednesday afternoon, but Ate sent me home after an hour. He said he didn't need help. Before I left, I found Mr. Black Bear by the main entrance, adjusting a crooked door.

"Nimo!" he said. "Heard your ate's trying to quit smoking. I used to smoke lots."

"Really?"

"Oh yeah," he nodded. "I still smoke sometimes."

"You do?"

"Yeah! I smoke when I have an electrical accident and set part of my clothes on fire."

"Uhm, okay, Mr. Black Bear," I said and started walking to my car outside. Before I drove off, I saw Ate by the dumpster, throwing cigarettes one by one into it.

After dinner, I did all the dishes. I looked out the kitchen window and saw Ate in the driveway. I shut the sink off and peeked into the living room, wondering if there would be another fight between him and Ina. Ate came in, threw a box of quit smoking patches on the carpet, and tossed his keys on the coffee table.

"You know I hate it when you throw things in the house," Ina said.

"I hate it when you leave bread crusts in the kitchen sink," Ate said.

"I really hate it when you don't shave. You look like a boy in weird puberty."

"Yeah? I hate it when you use my razor to shave your legs."

"I hate how you leave your dirty underwear on the bathroom floor."

"You know what I hate the most about you?" Ate answered as he rubbed his wedding ring. "I hate it when you don't talk to me. It kills me, Josie."

"You wanna know what I hate the most about you?" Ina went on. "I really hate it when you put your life at risk. You almost died when Nimo was a baby."

"How was I supposed to know I got a narrow aorta?" Ate said and raised his hands in the air. "See, you don't even got sense in your head."

"That's how I fell in love with you, you idiot," Ina said. "No matter how much crap you put me through, I love you, Jay Eagle. If you wanna keep smoking, go ahead, but you'll die before you turn 50 and it'll be because I killed you."

On Friday night, there was a football game against Custer High School from Sioux Plains. I played quarterback and Ignacio played noseguard. We barely won the game, but we still celebrated like hell in the locker room. When the rest of the team was in the showers, Ignacio swung off his sweaty jersey and John David froze up next to me.

"I can't hold it in anymore," he said. He walked over and popped the gay question. I closed my eyes, thinking Ignacio would punch John David in the face, but he laughed and said he'd answer the question later.

"Dammit Nimo, does everyone around here have to be straight?" John David said during our drive to Big Bat's for dinner after the game.

"You're not," I said.

"Real original, Nimo," he sighed. He reached into his backpack for his comb and he saw a note sticking out of his binder. John David read it out loud to me.

"Yes, I am. And I think you're really cute. Ignacio Puente," John David said. He told me to stop the car, so I pulled over. He got out of my car and did somersaults along the road. He hopped back inside after doing about ten.

At Big Bat's, John David couldn't stop squirming in his seat.

"He's gay!" he whispered to me. "And he thinks I'm cute!"

"John David, you barely even know him," I said right as Ignacio walked inside.

"There he is," John David said. "I'm going to ask him if he wants to date. This is gonna be so great, Nimo. Now I know how you feel when you see Cindy." He stood up from our booth and went to browse the candy aisle with Ignacio. They looked perfect for each other and I hoped Ignacio felt the same way for John David. As I watched them look over chocolate bars, Ate and Ina came in, holding hands.

"Congrats on the game, son," Ina said and dragged Ate to the service counter. They sat on barstools, talking and laughing from time to time. Ate rolled his shirt sleeve up to scratch his shoulder. He had a patch right under his tattoo of Ina's name.

The Diet

I loved being the quarterback for the Red Cloud High School Crusaders, but one day my parents got a letter from Coach Jumping Bull. It said I was too fat to keep playing. The whole team did a fitness test a week before and according to the guidelines, being a quarterback was dangerous with my weight.

"I'm a quarterback, I have to be big," I said to Ate and Ina during dinner.

"Might as well tell a stripper they're wearing too many clothes," Ate said.

"Jay Eagle, you're being filthy," Ina said. "I think we should all lose weight."

"We?" Ate said and chewed on his meat. "I didn't get no letter about being fat."

"We've all gained weight over the years," Ina said. "It's all this junk food we've been eating for so long. Starting tomorrow, we'll go on a diet and exercise routine. Nimo, instead of driving to school, ride your bike. This also means no more burgers or hot dogs at Big Bat's. The same goes for you, Jay Eagle."

"Me?" Ate gasped. "I work on my feet all day. I'm at the college waxing floors, washing windows, and fixing pipes. My job is a full cardio and weight lifting workout."

While they went on arguing about diets, I went to the garage and got on my bike. I pedaled to John David's house. Ignacio was with him on the porch. They whispered in Spanish so no one could understand them.

"Word is you're too fat to play," John David said.

"Shut up," I said. "What about you, Ignacio? What'd they say?"

"I'm healthy," he said. "But you're a quarterback, you gotta be big."

"I know," I shrugged. "They might as well send John David a letter saying he's checking out the cheerleaders too much."

"Aw man, how did you know?" John David said. "Don't worry about it, Nimo. I'm sure Coach Jumping Bull will put you back on the team in no time."

By breakfast time the next morning, Ina's diet plan was in full swing. Instead of my three bowls of sugary cereal and a sausage biscuit, I ate plain oatmeal and an apple.

"Josie, I can't eat this, I'm replacing windows today, I need some fuel," Ate said.

"Then put some gas in your mouth on your way to work," Ina told him. "Nimo, finish your oatmeal. It's got fiber."

"So do my clothes but I don't eat them," I said and she tugged me by my ponytail. I finished most of the oatmeal and started packing my usual lunch of a shredded beef sandwich with chips and a cookie until Ina stopped me.

"No more junk," Ina said. "You're taking a baked potato with a salad."

"Can I make the potato into French fries and put the salad in a burger?" I asked.

"Good one, Nimo," Ate said from the table, laughing.

"Jay Eagle, you're having the same thing," Ina said. "You've gotten pudgy." Ate stood up and told Ina to take back what she said. She poked him right in the belly button.

"Don't poke me, Josie," Ate said. Ina poked him again. Ate told her to stop, but she chased him into the living room and they fell on the couch together. While Ate yelled for her to get off, she kept poking him in the sides of his stomach.

"I'm gonna ride my bike to school," I said.

"Have a good day, Nimo," Ate said. "Josie, will you get off me?"

"Never," Ina said. They rolled themselves over and started making out. I rushed away as fast as I could.

When I got to school, I found John David patching a flat tire on his bike. Scott walked by us and said, "What happened to your bike, fruit salad? Did Nimo ride it?"

"No, but he did ride your mom last night," John David said. Scott swung a punch at him, but I stopped his fist in midair. He warned me to get out of his way and I reminded him that if I really wanted to, I could kill him.

"Dammit, you're right," Scott sighed as he looked at me up and down. "See ya."

In math class, I sat by Ignacio and he was working on a couple of problems he hadn't done for homework the night before.

"Why didn't you do them before you went to sleep?" I asked.

"Because I was doing something with JD before I went to sleep."

"Geez Ignacio, all night?" I said.

"No, not the whole night," he said. "I wasn't timing it, you freak." Mrs. Silver Hill started the lesson on scientific notation. She said it was useful for writing extremely large numbers and she asked Edmond Green Eyes to give her an example situation.

"Writing down Nimo's weight?" he said. I stood up waving my fists, but Ignacio pushed me down to my seat.

At lunch, I sat with John David and Ignacio, watching them chomp on greasy hot dogs while I was stuck eating a burnt potato with collard greens. I went to the cafeteria line to buy something decent. There was a big plate of chocolate chip cookies for 25 cents each. I grabbed the last one. I walked back to my table and I overheard two girls behind me say, "Nimo bought all the cookies – can you believe his tubby butt?"

"My butt's real, I don't have to stuff my underwear with toilet paper," I said to them. John David and Ignacio laughed and the girls called us perverts.

"How does everything get around this rez so fast?" I asked after the girls left.

"Contain yourself," John David said. "Being fat doesn't make you an asshole."

"Yeah," Ignacio said. "Everyone's got something other people will make fun of."

"Did you know Iggy's got a big birthmark on his butt and it looks just like a rocket ship?" John David said and Ignacio playfully told him to shut up. Until John David started dating Ignacio, I never saw him happier. He was usually as much of a stone face as Mount Rushmore, always trying to be tough, focused on weight lifting and building up his stamina. When Ignacio came to Pine Ridge, John David changed, but not drastically, just differently. Even though John David and

Ignacio were happy together, the only ones who knew they were a couple were my parents, Miss Running Bear, and me. I wished their relationship didn't have to be a secret.

A week passed since I was out on the football field and I was restless. I stopped by Spotted Elk College and asked Ate if he could schedule me to work more hours, but he wanted me focusing on school. I told him I wanted to save more money to see Cindy Blackbird in Los Angeles. We only saw each other three or four times a year, but we talked on the phone every day. I was set to see her during winter break and I planned to take her out as much as I could.

"Your hours are fine, hoksila," Ate said as he installed a new doorknob for a classroom. "Why don't you use your extra time to exercise?"

"Football was my exercise," I said. "I haven't seen Cindy since June, maybe she'll think I'm too fat when I see her in December."

"Nimo," Ate said and stood up. "Let me tell you something my tunkasila James Eagle told me when I was about your age."

"If it's about doing it, using protection, or boners, you've told me."

"Nimo, you're being filthy," Ate said. "Anyway, my tunkasila James Eagle was a big man. For most of his life, he weighed about 300 pounds. But my unci Isabella loved every pound of him. He said to me, 'Jay Eagle, one day you're gonna get married and if your wife's a good cook, you're gonna get fat. If she tells you you're too fat and leaves you, you find her and sit on her.'"

"Ate, I'm going home," I said.

"I ain't finished yet," Ate went on. "If your wife tells you're too fat and she makes you a salad, that means she loves your big, fat butt and you eat that damn awful salad with a smile on your face."

"Who eats a salad with a smile on their face, Ate?"

"I don't know, Nimo, just go home," Ate said and patted my back. I walked to my bike outside and I rode a couple laps around the parking lot. Afterwards, I rode around the rez going nowhere in particular, but I couldn't avoid Ray Firebird. He asked me in his slurred voice why I was cut from the Crusaders if I wasn't too fat.

"Coach Jumping Bull thinks I might have a heart attack if I play," I said.

"You should try jumping in front of people like me. I'm in great shape." He took his shirt off. He flexed his flabby arms and did a few belly rolls.

"I'll keep it in mind," I said, holding back my gags.

When I got home, it was past dinnertime and I was sweating all over my body. Ina told me my plate of cranberry salad with grilled chicken breast was in the fridge.

"I'll skip dinner tonight, I'm too tired to eat," I said, panting.

"You'll skip dinner? Ina slaved away in the kitchen cooking for us," Ate said.

"Jay Eagle, I bought the salad at Sioux Nation and the chicken's leftover from last night, you need your head examined. And Nimo, you need a shower."

"I know," I said and went to the bathroom. I swung my soaked shirt off and looked in the mirror. My big belly sagged over my waistline.

After not being on the football field for almost a month, I asked Ignacio if he wanted to exercise with me on days he didn't have practice. Ignacio planned to study kinesiology in college and he once said his dream job was to be a personal trainer. On our first day of exercise, we went to the park by Red Cloud High School. Ignacio made me run a mile, do 50 pushups and sit ups, 30 jumping jacks, and sprint for two minutes.

"Looks like you got a good workout in," he said to me while I sprawled on the ground. "You're really sweaty."

"That's only half sweat," I said. "The other half is my tears."

"Good, that's very good," he nodded. Ignacio bent down to me and he helped me stand without struggling at all since he was always much stronger than me.

"Hey Ignacio, have you ever made John David workout this hard?" I panted.

"Yeah," Ignacio said. "But he's done way more intense than what you just did."

"Geez, what'd you have him do?"

"Me," he said with a laugh. I turned my head to the side and gagged.

"C'mon Nimo, it's not like you don't have sex with Cindy," Ignacio said.

"I don't."

"You don't? I thought she was your girlfriend," he said.

"No, we're still just friends. I like her a lot, but I'm too fat for her."

"Don't say that," he told me. "Love is worth more than someone's weight."

"Yeah, you're right," I said. "I never thought I'd get girl advice from my gay friend, to be honest with you." Ignacio put an arm around me.

"You know what they say about the gays," he said, laughing.

"We have special powers nobody else does. Not making kids is one of them."

When I got home, Leksi Gray Mountain was lying on the couch, watching TV. He came to Pine Ridge every Friday to volunteer at the Indian Health Service Clinic and sometimes he slept over so he wouldn't have to drive all the way back to Sioux Plains. He asked me why I had been cut from the football team.

"How did you know?" I asked.

"Your coach has erectile dysfunction and he came to see me today and he told me," Leksi said. "He said it was something about you being overweight."

"Yeah," I sighed. "But I was quarterback, I'm supposed to be big."

"Nimo, that's ridiculous. I've looked through your medical records and sure, you need to lose some weight, but everything else about you is good. How about I give you a note that says you're a hundred percent healthy enough to play football?"

"Gray Mountain, isn't that malpractice?" Ina said from the kitchen.

"The hell with malpractice, Josie," Ate answered from the bathroom. "Malpractice was the US government making Mount Rushmore; it's about time we lied too. You give Nimo the note, ciye."

"I'll take it, Leksi," I said. He scribbled down I was a healthy teenager and signed it 'Dr. Gray M. Thunderclap.'

On Tuesday afternoon, I showed up to football practice and gave Coach Jumping Bull the note.

"The doctor who wrote this note is your uncle, Nimo. I can't give this to the school board," Coach Jumping Bull said.

"They'll think I'm up to something."

"My uncle says you can't get anything up right now," I said. He told me to shut up and get out on the field. I joined the other Crusaders, relieved.

When practice was over, I went to the locker room to shower and change. The rest of the team had already gone home. It was only me, Ignacio, and John David. John David was busy putting all the dirty towels in a hamper.

"Geez Iggy, you smell like a dead skunk," John David said.

"I've been out in the sun for two hours," Ignacio said.

"Grass has been out in the sun since the beginning of time and it doesn't stink half as bad as you do," John David said and handed us clean towels. Ignacio swung his #59 jersey off and wiped his bare chest with it.

"Mind if I join you for your shower?" John David said to Ignacio with a wink.

"Guys," I said.

"Nimo, there's room for one more," John David said and I stuck my tongue out.

By the time I rode my bike home, it was dark and I couldn't see very well. About half a mile before I got to my neighborhood, a truck flashed its lights behind me. I pulled over to the side to let it pass, but it pulled over with me.

"Nimo!" Ina said. "It's pitch black out here, load your bike on the truck!"

"But you told me to ride my bike from now on," I said.

"Not when it's this dark, hoksila," Ate said. I put my bike on the truck's bed and slid into the backseat. Ina asked Ate how his doctor's appointment went earlier that day.

"Doc says to watch my sugar intake and my weight so I don't get diabetes," he said and then parked on our driveway. "My

114

heart is doing good, so there's that. Nimo, you also gotta watch your sugar and weight. Diabetes is rampant in the Thunderclap family."

"Jay Eagle, if you ever get diabetes, it'll be because you're too sweet," Ina said and kissed him on his right cheek. Even though it was dark, I could see Ate blushing.

After dinner, I changed into my sleeping clothes and threw myself on my bed. It was still early in Los Angeles so I called Cindy. Her phone rang seven times before she finally answered. I never got tired of hearing her voice.

"Hey beautiful," I said. "I'm about to go to bed, but I wanted to say goodnight."

"Nimo," she said. "It's only 70 more days until you come down to see me."

"Yeah, I know," I said. "I'm counting the days down. Oh, uh, I've put on some weight, but I'm trying to lose it before I see you."

"Nimo, do me a favor," Cindy said. "Don't lose too much. I wanna rub your tummy as soon as you get here." I promised I'd keep my stomach, mostly because it was attached to my body. I said goodnight to Cindy and turned my light off. I couldn't stop thinking about her eyes. She had brown eyes like me, but her left one was lazy. I met Cindy when I was 13 at the Los Angeles Pow Wow and she had her left eye totally covered with her long, black hair. I asked her to pull her hair back because I wanted to see all of her face.

"My left eye is lazy," she said. "It looks like I'm falling asleep."

"If I were your eye, I'd get really tired too. It must take a lot of work to be beautiful every day," I said.

"You think I'm beautiful?" she said.

"Of course," I said. "I know beautiful when I see it." I asked her if I could give her a hug and she nodded. I put my arms around her and she patted me on my stomach.

The Burst

*I*gnacio was voted Best Looking Crusader by a poll in the school newspaper and he was asked out on a date by almost every girl in our grade. Like John David did before him, he turned all the girls down.

"I swear to God, Nimo, if one more girl asks me out, I'm gonna burst," Ignacio said to me one afternoon when we were in the locker room.

"Yeah, it must be terrible to have so many ladies after you," I said, rolling my eyes. "You wanna grab some dinner? I could go for Big Bat's." Ignacio shook his head. The Homecoming Game was the next day and he wanted to rest for it. He said his stomach was hurting and he wasn't hungry anyway, which was unusual for him since he was always snacking on some kind of fruit or vegetable. He headed home and I went to Big Bat's with John David instead.

"That's weird, he never gets sick," John David said while we ate. "If his parents weren't such assholes, I'd go check on him." John David had been openly gay for around two years. The Puentes didn't know Ignacio was also gay, but they didn't like him hanging around John David because they thought Ignacio could 'catch the gay bug.'

"Do you guys ever get sick of sneaking around?" I asked.

"Sometimes," John David shrugged. "But when you sneak around, it makes your sex life awesome. We do it almost every day."

"Geez, John David," I said and took a big bite of my burger.

"Lighten up, Nimo," John David said. "I don't only like Ignacio for his body. I like him for other reasons, too."

"Like what?" I asked.

"Everything," he answered. "He's funny, he's nice, he's caring, oh for God's sake, Nimo, you're making me sound like a dumb soap opera here." John David got up to grab his slushy order from the counter. As he walked back to our table, Scott and his buddies, Joshua Redshirt and Mark Greenwood, threw paper airplanes at his head. They snickered to each other, whispering "Fruitcake," "Sissy," and "Queer." John David gave them the middle finger. At first, they shut up, but they started again a few minutes later.

"Scott, I told you to stop!" Claudia called out from the counter. "If you keep saying those things, I'm gonna find another boyfriend!" All of Big Bat's turned to Scott. Mr. and Mrs. Graywolf applauded. The other customers pointed at Scott, including me and John David. Scott puffed up his chest, walked to John David, and shook his hand.

"This is just so I can keep my girl," he said. "I bet you wish you could date me."

"Scott, sorry to tell you this, but I'm into men," John David said. The rest of Big Bat's exploded in laughs. Scott and his buddies left right away with Claudia chasing after them. I high fived John David three times.

"Those idiots always pick on you. I'm sick of it."

"They're all talk," John David said, shaking his head. "It's not like they're gonna beat me up or something for being gay. They only wanna look tough."

On the morning of the Homecoming Game, Ignacio threw up in the bathroom right before the first bell rang.

"I haven't thrown up in years," he said and clutched his stomach.

"I know what it is," I said and lightly poked his stomach. "You're pregnant!"

"Shut up, Nimo, me and JD use protection," he told me. Ever since the first time I met him, Ignacio was strong as an ox and looked like he could instantly crush me with his pinkie finger. It was so strange to see him pale, shaky, and weak.

At lunch, Ignacio didn't eat anything. He usually ate his own healthy snacks, bought lunch from the cafeteria, and ate some of John David's lunch too. I offered him my bag of chips, but he didn't take it.

"I'm not hungry," Ignacio said. "And I still don't feel good."

"That's it, I'm taking you to the nurse's office," John David said and tugged at Ignacio's arm. Ignacio and John David were about the same height, but Ignacio was way more muscular. John David couldn't budge him at all. Mr. Puente used to be a heavyweight boxer in Puerto Rico, years before he became a pastor. He was even taller and heavier than Ignacio and he wore an eye patch because he lost his right eye in a fight. Sometimes I worried about him discovering Ignacio and John David were together. He could probably kill them both with one punch.

"We got the game tonight," Ignacio said. "Nimo, gimme

those chips, I can't play on an empty stomach." I handed him the chips. He never opened them.

The Homecoming Game was against the Beresford High School Watchdogs. They kicked our asses several times in the past, but that was before Ignacio started playing. An hour before the game, Ignacio and me were in the locker room, changing into our jerseys, and he could barely move.

"It hurts, Nimo, it really hurts," he said and held onto his stomach.

"If you're in that much pain, you need to sit out," I said. "Don't worry about the game. We win some, we lose some."

"We haven't lost any since I started playing," he groaned, holding his stomach.

When all the other players were gone, John David got a wet towel for Ignacio. He patted it on Ignacio's forehead and he gave him small, quick kisses. I stayed by the door to make sure nobody else saw them.

Out on the field, I sat next to Ignacio, watching the cheer-leaders do their routine. All the other players had their eyes on the cheerleaders, including Scott. He whistled at them and talked about how sexy they were.

"Scott, you're with Claudia," I reminded him.

"That don't mean I can't look," he shrugged. "Check out Katelyn, Ignacio. Word is she wants to ask you out."

"I see her," Ignacio answered, even though he was looking at his shoes. Soon after the routine, it was time to play. I stood up, but Ignacio stayed on the bench.

"Nimo," he said. "I really don't feel good. Get some help."

"Hey, if you're gonna puke again, please don't do it on me," I said and stepped away from him. He collapsed off the bench and landed on the ground.

Ignacio was rushed to the IHS Hospital. The game went on, but I didn't play and John David wasn't there with towels and water. We lost miserably at a score of 7-42. Ate and Ina took me to the hospital. They never missed any of my games. Their favorite thing to do was bad mouth the other team's quarterback. When we got to IHS, they took turns hugging me and telling me they loved me.

"I hope Ignacio's okay," Ina said as she held me. "He's your age, Nimo. That's way too young to die."

"Would you quit being so negative?" Ate said. "He might not even die, maybe he'll just be a vegetable. It can't be too bad to be a piece of broccoli."

"His stomach blew up, Jay Eagle, he might not ever eat again," Ina said. "Poor thing. No more Big Bat's food for him if he's not okay."

I wiggled myself out of Ina's grasp and told her I was going to grab some dinner at the hospital's café. They didn't hear me since they were still arguing about how bad Ignacio was doing.

I found John David at the café, sticking a fork in and out of some chopped carrots. He had a plate of chicken breast and potato salad next to the carrots, but he hadn't touched anything. He pushed the plate to me. I took a big bite out of the chicken breast and it was ice cold.

"I ran into Mr. Puente earlier," he said, still picking at his carrots. "Damn pirate didn't tell me anything about Ignacio. But I saw your leksi and he said he'd find out what's wrong for me."

"Mr. Puente can be nice," I said. "Well, I guess he's nice to people who aren't gay. Sorry, John David."

"Nimo, something's really bothering me," John David said

and pushed his stabbed carrots aside. He moved his eyes to the television hanging in the corner of the café, showing a rerun of All in the Family.

"I think I love Ignacio," he said, still looking at the television.

"Why is that bad?"

"I can't ever be with him for good," he went on. "We have to sneak around from his parents, especially his ate. I wish we could date like everyone else, you know, get dinner at Big Bat's or go to the park and not worry about what people think. We can't even get married in this state. But damn it, he's the best thing that ever happened to me."

"Never thought I'd see the day you fell in love," I said. He groaned loudly.

"I hate that word," he said. "Love. It sounds like something people say right before they puke everywhere."

"It's not all bad," I said. "My parents still love each other."

"I'm not lovey dovey. Even Valentine's Day makes me sick. I don't know what it is about Iggy, he makes me feel things I thought I would never, ever feel about anyone."

John David and me spent the rest of the night in the waiting area, catching up on homework. Ate and Ina fell asleep in each other's arms on a couch across from us. Leksi finally came by around midnight. Ignacio's appendix burst and he needed emergency surgery, but he was going to be okay.

"I just sewed him up, he should be back to normal by next week," Leksi said and patted me on the head. "I'm gonna sleep at your house tonight, Nimo. You guys can visit for a couple minutes, but he's still woozy. Let him rest if he needs to."

John David walked into Ignacio's room before I did and he hunched down next to him, whispering in his ear and rubbing his hand. Ignacio opened his eyes about halfway.

"Did we win?" he asked me, almost asleep.

"I have no idea," I lied.

"Don't worry about it too much, Iggy," John David said and stroked Ignacio's forehead. "You scored right before you passed out."

"JD, don't talk about our sex life in front of Nimo," Ignacio said. John David laughed a little. Ignacio said something more, but he was so groggy, neither of us understood him. John David gave Ignacio a quick kiss on his lips.

"I love you, Iggy," John David whispered. We started walking out of the room and we heard Ignacio grumble, "I love you too, JD."

Ignacio stayed in the hospital for the whole weekend. John David wanted to visit him on Saturday, but he waited until Sunday morning, when the Puentes were busy at church. They owned the Temple of God's Love on Sundance Road. Mr. Puente was the head pastor and Mrs. Puente was the director of the church preschool, but sometimes she preached. I went to the Temple of God's Love once and Mr. Puente badmouthed gay men during the entire sermon. But I didn't hate the Puentes. When they were missionaries, they were always there for me, my family, and anyone else who needed help.

"JD is taking his sweet time," Ignacio said while we waited for John David.

"He hasn't been getting much sleep since you've been in here," I said.

"Damn," Ignacio said. "He hates missing even one minute of sleep. I wish I could have seen him yesterday, but I didn't know my parents were gonna be here all day long."

We watched a daytime talk show on his room's tiny TV. The

talk show was about sex problems – too much cheating, not enough intimacy, and paternity. Ignacio looked at me and he said was relieved he'd never have a paternity suit. John David finally walked in close to noon. He shut the door behind him and gave Ignacio kisses on his forehead.

"Sorry I'm late," John David said. "Ray Firebird jumped in front of my truck."

"I thought you forgot about me," Ignacio told John David.

"Have you eaten yet?" John David asked him. "I can grab something for you. I was gonna go to Big Bat's for some hot dogs, but I wasn't sure if you could eat them right now. What do you want me to get for you?"

"Pancakes would be good I guess," Ignacio said. John David left the room and I stayed behind with Ignacio, telling him the full details of how we 'won' the game against the Watchdogs.

"I can't wait to play again," he said. "I'm so tired of this place. I keep getting stripped, poked, and touched. It feels way better when JD does all those things to me."

"He's been really worried about you," I said.

"Poor guy," Ignacio answered and stretched his arms. "I've never felt so important to anyone before, except Coach Jumping Bull. Can I tell you something?"

"You're pregnant?" I said.

"Of course not," he said. "I'm in love with JD, but I don't know if he feels the same way about me."

"You guys have been together for a year, why wouldn't he?" I asked.

"I've been waiting for the perfect time to tell him," he said. I didn't mention he already told John David the night before.

"JD isn't a softie," Ignacio continued. "He hates love songs, romantic movies, and Valentine's Day. He's not into love, maybe since his parents broke up. I don't know how to tell him I love him. He'll think I'm joking or he'll probably think it's gross."

"I don't think so," I said. "He's not a softie, but it doesn't mean he doesn't have feelings. Go ahead and tell him. If he doesn't feel the same way, all he's going to do is call you something ugly and pretend like the conversation never happened."

After half an hour, John David was finally back with a stack of pancakes drowning in syrup. I excused myself to the bathroom in the corner to give them privacy.

"Rumor is you love me," I heard Ignacio say.

"Those damn tabloids," John David said. "All right, I do. Now put me in front of a firing squad and let's pretend this talk never happened." I stepped out of the bathroom and saw John David cutting the stack of pancakes into little pieces. He fed each one to Ignacio. When the pancakes were gone, Ignacio leaned over to John David and kissed him on his left cheek.

"Geez Iggy, you got syrup on me," John David said and he wiped the sticky residue off with a napkin.

"Sorry, my love," Ignacio said. John David looked at him and for a minute or so, he didn't move. He rubbed Ignacio's forehead and he asked him to never burst any part of his body again.

"I won't," Ignacio said, holding onto John David's hand. "I love you, JD."

"Iggy, you're gonna make me puke."

"Lots of people love each other, there's nothing to be afraid of. Do you love me back?" Ignacio said. John David threw himself on the chair next to Ignacio's bed. Sweat poured out of his forehead. This was a guy who could lift up a 300-pound barbell, run two miles in less than ten minutes, and swim for an hour without stopping for a break. But one mention of love got him so weak kneed, he couldn't stand up.

"I love you too, Iggy," John David finally said. "I've never felt this way before. I thought it was indigestion or something."

"I love you," Ignacio told him and reached an arm around him. He kissed John David's cheek. "Hey Nimo, thanks for not calling us gross."

"No problem," I said. "The only people I find gross are my parents."

At one in the afternoon, when Ignacio's parents were on their way, John David and me rushed out of Ignacio's room. Right when we go to the parking lot, we saw Mr. Puente coming towards us and he was adjusting his eye patch. Mrs. Puente was behind him, pushing him along. John David dived between two minivans.

"Nimo!" Mrs. Puente said. She ran to me and hugged me. "It's always so good to see you. You've grown up so much over the years. It's so wonderful to see how Jesus has been so good to you and your family."

"You need to tell your sissy friend about Jesus," Mr. Puente said. Mrs. Puente smacked his arm.

"Did you visit Ignacio?" Mr. Puente said, still fiddling with his eye patch.

"Oh yeah, we had some pancakes and watched TV," I said. "He seems to be all better now. Maybe he'll be back on the football field next week."

"Thanks for spending time with him, Nimo," Mrs. Puente said. "You're such a nice boy. I'm glad Ignacio's got you as a friend."

"Did the faggot come by?" Mr. Puente asked me. I shook my head.

"Antonio, John David is still a child of God," Mrs. Puente said.

"If he was a child of God, he wouldn't be a faggot," he answered with a loud grunt.

"Antonio, is that something Jesus would say?" she asked him. He didn't answer her. Mrs. Puente gave me another hug and a quick kiss on my forehead. She asked Jesus to bless me and Mr. Puente kept on grunting. Then the Puentes walked into the hospital, but they weren't holding hands like my parents always did.

"Are you sure they didn't see me?" John David said when they were gone.

"I'm sure," I said.

"Of course they didn't, I was hiding behind your giant butt," John David said with a laugh. He walked to his truck, looking over his shoulder after every couple of steps.

Until Ignacio was finally up and about again, the Crusaders lost two more games. We still needed to play against the Willow Lake High School Pirates, but if we lost to them, our team wouldn't qualify for the championship game.

"They're called the Pirates?" John David said to me as he folded towels for the game against Willow Lake. "Mr. Puente can be their mascot."

"C'mon John David, he's not so bad," I said, but he wasn't the nicest person in the world either. Sometimes I thought Mr. Puente didn't really lose his eye in a fight, but someone got mad at him and gouged it out.

"He needs someone to take out his second eye," John David said. "Actually, no, he needs somebody to take out his mouth so he can shut up forever."

"He's still Ignacio's ate. If you guys can ever get married in the future, he'll be your ate in law."

"Sometimes you gotta break the law," John David said. He placed all the folded towels onto a rolling cart and headed out to the field.

Even though it looked like the Pirates were going to whoop us in the first half of the game, we beat them by two points. Ignacio was drained by the end and he dragged himself to the locker room, too weak to take his jersey off.

"I should've stayed home," he panted heavily. "You guys didn't need me tonight, you still won."

"You did most of the work," I said. I was surprised he hadn't collapsed again. After about half an hour, the rest of the team was out of the locker room and I got my stuff together to head home. John David emerged from the back with a long, warm towel.

"You reek, Iggy," John David said. "I could smell you from the storage room."

"Yeah, I know," Ignacio said. "I'm freezing." John David sat down next to him. He gently wrapped the towel around Ignacio's shivering body.

The Crush

"Geez, Nimo, would you just ask her out already?" John David said. "You're gonna give yourself a heart attack." We were at Big Bat's, eating hot dogs and French fries. I had just found out Cindy was coming to see me for Christmas break. We had been friends for almost four years and my crush for her grew more and more. I always wanted her to be my girlfriend, but I didn't know if she liked me back.

"What if she doesn't like me?" I said.

"She's coming up here right?" he asked. "If she didn't like you, she wouldn't bother to see you at all. Surprise her with something nice."

"Like what?" I shrugged.

"Nimo, I'm gay, I don't know how to woo the ladies," he said. I admit I was a little jealous of John David's relationship with Ignacio. They were so close and loving to each other. They were both handsome and they could get any girl at school they wanted if they were straight. Girls probably wished I was gay so I'd quit asking them out.

"Cindy's a really pretty girl," I said. "I bet she's got 1,000 guys lined up all over LA waiting to date her. When she comes up here, she'll have another 1,000 guys after her. She could have any guy she wants. Why would she want me?"

"She's not gonna want you if you keep whining," John David said. "Be the Nimo you always are. If you start acting different, she'll like the other Nimo instead and that's not the real Nimo."

"Who is the real Nimo?"

"The one who doesn't ask Cindy out," he said. "Actually, you might wanna be a different Nimo from now on."

Cindy arrived in South Dakota for Christmas vacation a couple weeks later. She was Apache, White Mountain to be exact. When I saw her walking towards me at the Rapid City Regional Airport, I wanted to hide because, as Ate would say it, I built a teepee in my pants.

"Quick Nimo, think about Ray Firebird naked," Ate whispered in my ear. His advice solved the problem faster than I thought.

"You really like this girl, huh?" Ate asked and I nodded.

"How cute," Ate said. "I remember the first time I saw your ina. She was so beautiful, I thought I was dreaming. Those eyes, her face, her hair behind-"

"Ate, I don't need to know."

"I was gonna say her hair behind her shoulders. Now you got me thinking me about your ina's behind. I'm about to have a teepee in my pants along with you."

"Oh man," I said, burying my face in my hands.

"Nimo!" Cindy said when she finally reached me. She swung her arms around me and I looked at Ate with sweat drizzling down my forehead. Ray Firebird naked, he mouthed. Ray Firebird in a thong.

We started the two hour drive to Pine Ridge after Cindy got the rest of her luggage. Ate drove us and I sat in the backseat with Cindy. She told me a guy at her high school asked her out the week before, but she turned him down. I asked her why and she said he smelled funny. Right then, I took a deep breath to smell myself.

"What about you, Nimo? Has anyone asked you out?"

"Me?" I said. "No, I've been too busy with football and stuff." Ate stared at me through the rearview mirror, so I changed my answer to "And you know I work, so I only wanna date someone special," which still sounded dumb to me.

"That's so sweet," Cindy said and Ate gave me a thumbs up. I didn't know exactly how I'd date Cindy with her living in Los Angeles, but if she wanted to be my girlfriend, I would hitchhike or stowaway in a train if I needed to.

When Ate pulled up to our house, I saw John David and Ignacio parked in our driveway. I walked Cindy inside and then I went back out to see what they wanted.

"We wanna meet her," Ignacio said.

"C'mon guys, can't you wait?" I said.

"No," John David answered. "We need to embarrass you because that's what friends do." I told John David and Ignacio to go away, but they started making loud kissing noises at me. I gave in and said they could come inside. Since it was dark and thick snow was coming down, they held hands as they walked to the door.

At dinner, I sat next to Cindy with my legs shaking and my heart pounding.

"Cindy, how's the City of Angels?" Ate asked as he scooped mashed potatoes.

"Good, Mr. Thunderclap. My dad just opened a print shop near the airport. If it goes well, he wants to open more locations. His grocery stores are doing well, too."

"How fancy," Ina said. "Did you know Nimo likes to write? Maybe he can print some stuff out at your dad's shop next time he's down there." I got up from the table to get more juice and John David started telling Cindy about how I had a short story published in the school newspaper and how much everybody liked it. Cindy asked me if she could read it and I said I didn't have any extra copies of the paper.

"I have tons in my truck," John David said. "If you want more, you should make some copies with Cindy at her dad's shop."

"Hey John David, I think I left something in your truck," I said and he followed me out to the driveway. We stood at his truck, shivering.

"I'm dying in there," I said. "I can't even look at her."

"She is a pretty girl. And that's coming from a gay dude."

"Every time I look at her, I get a hard on," I said and put a hand over my face. "What if she notices? She'll think I'm a jerk."

"Nimo, I'm sure she likes you and wants to be your girlfriend, all you need to do is ask her." I nodded and stuck my hands in my pockets, trying to warm them.

"Hey, what made you have a crush on Ignacio?" I asked with my teeth chattering from all the cold winds blowing my way.

"Uh," John David said. "He's freaking hot and I wanted to hit it."

"You want me to go back in there and say, 'hi Cindy, I wanna hit it'?" I asked, which made John David almost fall over from laughing. He said he'd give me twenty dollars if I actually did, but I begged him to give me a serious answer.

"Okay," he went on after he got the last of his laughs out. "When Ignacio took me on our first date, we had to get some groceries for his parents. We went to Sioux Nation and while we were in the aisles, he called me his husband and we pretended we were married. It was the best grocery shopping ever."

Cindy was only going to be in Pine Ridge for a week. I had to ask her out quick. I took her to Big Bat's for hot dogs and drinks and she reminded me she didn't eat meat. She fell in love with animals after reading Charlotte's Web in 3rd grade. She had told me she was a vegetarian several times. It was my fault for forgetting.

"You can have mine," she said.

"No, I'm not hungry anymore." We sat down by the window, watching people pump gas into their cars.

"It's amazing how we're almost done with high school, don't you think? And since you already work now, it will be easier for you to get a good job after you graduate," she said. Cindy was a year younger than me, but she was old enough to work, except she didn't have to since her dad was rich. Compared to her, the money I earned was nothing. Mr. Blackbird had five small grocery stores around Los Angeles and he planned to open five more within the next few years and now he had a print shop, too. He alone probably made five or six times the amount of money my parents did together.

"Hey Nimo!" Mr. Graywolf said. "Is this your girlfriend?"

"No!" I said, way too loud. "This is Cindy. She's the girl I met at the LA Pow Wow a couple years ago. This is her first time visiting Pine Ridge."

"Welcome to the rez," Mr. Graywolf said as he shook her hand. "My wife makes the best hot dogs and hamburgers in the whole state. I'll give you some on the house."

"Thank you," Cindy said. "But I don't eat meat."

"No meat?" he said. "There ain't any meat in California? No wonder there's earthquakes – it's probably from all the people rioting for some steaks."

I ended up taking the hot dog and hamburger in a to-go box for myself. After Big Bat's, we went to Sioux Nation to get some bread and eggs. We saw John David and Ignacio by the juice, but they didn't see us right away. They were whispering, like they usually did in public.

"Have you asked her out yet?" Ignacio whispered to me while Cindy and John David talked about the best kind of orange juice.

"I forgot she doesn't eat meat and I just took her out for hot dogs at Big Bat's. I'm gonna wait until she doesn't think I'm an asshole."

"Lighten up," Ignacio said. "She might like you back."

"I've never had a girlfriend before," I shrugged.

"Me either," he said with a smile.

"Real funny, Ignacio," I said. When John David was done with his orange juice speech, I took Cindy to the candy aisle and asked her to choose her favorite. She picked up a bag of gummy worms.

"I know you like these a lot," she said with her face close to mine. "I'll buy them for you. Think of them as an early Christmas gift."

"Yeah, I sure do like," I said, stuttering. "Uh, gummy worms."

Cindy and I drove back to my house through more snow. We passed families shoveling their driveways, kids throwing snowballs, and Ray Firebird doing some weird kind of dance to stay warm. I felt Cindy shiver next to me. The heat in my car didn't work very well. When Unci was still alive, she always said she'd fix it, but she never did. I was used to minimal heat since I didn't have a lot of it as a kid. When temperatures dropped lower than usual, Ate burned some of his carvings to warm the trailer. He hated having to destroy his own art. If he didn't, we could have frozen to death. Cindy, on the other hand, grew up in sunny Los Angeles. She couldn't take the cold anymore.

"Nimo," she said. "It is freezing. Are we almost there?"

"Just one more street," I said. "Here, take my coat." I swung it off and gave it to her. She wrapped my big coat around her small body tightly. She looked adorable.

Before dinner, I sat by the fireplace with Ate, watching him carve a cane for Mrs. Yellow Fire's mother in law. Cindy and Ina were in the kitchen, making dinner. I asked Ate how he got Ina to like him when they were first dating.

"Oh Nimo," he said. "I'm still trying to get my special lady to like me."

"Special lady? Who is she?" Ina asked as she walked into the living room.

"My lover, Scarlett Blue Bird, she says hi," Ate answered.

"That's sweet of her," Ina said. "My lover Lawrence Red Horse says hi to you."

"What do you say we go on a double date this weekend?" Ate asked Ina.

"That's a good idea," Ina said. "I know you and Lawrence would get along great. Food's hot and ready. Come eat it before the weather freezes it back up."

We had plates of frybread slices, Caesar salad, and bean stew. Cindy kept complimenting Ina on her cooking. I didn't hear all of what she told her. I couldn't stop myself from looking at her beautiful face.

"Nimo, would you pass the damn frybread? I'm starving

here!" Ate said and slammed his hands on the table.

"Sorry," I said when I came back to reality. I quickly slid the plate to him. Cindy patted my hand when she was finished eating. I watched her get up and take her empty plate to the sink. No matter how cold it was outside, I felt warm looking at Cindy.

After dinner, I asked Cindy if she wanted dessert. She said my ina hadn't made any, but I told her I'd make her whatever she wanted. She asked for ice cream with cookie pieces and marshmallows on top. There was plenty of ice cream and marshmallows, but the only cookies I found were Ate's SuperFiberMan cookies.

"Why I can't have those cookies?" Cindy asked me when I served her dessert.

"You don't need those, you have a beautiful digestive system," I said, wishing I kept my dumb mouth shut.

"I do?" she said with a laugh. "Have you seen it?"

"No, but the rest of you is beautiful, so I'm guessing all of your organs are too."

"This ice cream is delicious," she said. "There's a new ice cream place down the street from my house. Next time you come to LA, I'll take you there. It's all handmade ice cream and it's not super sweet, but just right."

"Like you," I blurted. She blushed and rubbed my left cheek.

"I'm gonna go to bed now," she said as she stretched her arms up. "Goodnight, Nimo." She stood up and bent down to my face. I thought she was going to kiss my cheek. Instead, she patted my shoulder.

While she washed up in the bathroom, I went to the guest bedroom. I straightened out the blankets, fluffed the pillows, and left a note for her on the nightstand. Goodnight Cindy.

Get your unneeded beauty sleep. Nimo.

Cindy was still dreaming when we all got up at 7 am the next morning. Ate shoveled snow off the driveway and Ina made hot chocolate in the kitchen. I took over stirring the hot chocolate while she fried eggs for breakfast.

"Ina," I asked her through the sizzles. "How did you and Ate get together?"

"He followed me home and your grandparents said I could keep him."

"C'mon Ina," I sighed. Ina leaned over and kissed my forehead.

"You know how I used to be a dancer, right?" she went on. "At the 1983 Sioux Plains Pow Wow, I was doing my usual routine and I hurt my ankle. I went to rest by the food stands and Ate was there wiping the tables. He was so cute, Nimo. I wanted to kiss him right away."

"You liked Ate 'cause he was cute?" I said. If being cute was the only way to get a girl, I figured I'd quit trying.

"No," Ina said as she turned the eggs over. "Your ate was really cute but what kept me with him was how sweet he was. Before one of our dates, I caught the flu, and I called him to cancel. He woke me up from my nap a few hours later and he had gotten me orange juice, soup, vitamins, and a teddy bear. Then we started making out and your grandparents yelled at us. Anyway, there was lots of boys who wanted to go out with me but they all sucked. The only one who didn't was Ate."

"All right Josie, the driveway's clear!" Ate said when he walked into the kitchen, shivering. "You'd do a way better job getting rid of snow. You're so hot, you can just stand outside for a minute and it will all melt."

"Oh Jay Eagle, I've already caused enough global warming," Ina said. Ate put his arms around her and held her until the eggs were ready.

In the afternoon, I took Cindy to John David's house. He needed help wrapping gifts for the annual toy drive. After the toys were ready, I helped him load them into his truck. He was taking them to the Temple of God's Love, even though Mr. Puente hated seeing him there.

"The toy distribution's at seven," he said when we finished loading. "Ignacio said his parents need someone to play Santa and I told them you'd do it."

"What if I screw it up?" I said.

"Nimo, you sit in a chair, listen to the kids whine, and hand them a gift."

"Why can't you do it then?"

"Because you're," John David said and fiddled with his hands. "Uh, more Santa shaped than I am." At first, I wanted to punch him, but he was right. Cindy offered to be Mrs. Claus when I told her about it. We got in my car and followed John David to the Temple of God's Love. During the drive, she told me about a crazy dream she had the night before. She said we were in my car and we went to Mount Rushmore. When we got there, I started holding her hand and I wouldn't let it go.

"Like this?" I asked and took her hand in mine when we came to a red light.

"Yeah," Cindy said. "And you told me I was pretty." She held my hand tighter. She didn't let go until we parked at the church.

After fitting into the Santa outfit, I sat in a chair with Cindy by my side, waiting for the kids. The first one to come up was Scott. I told him he was too old for Santa, but he sat down on my lap anyway.

"I don't want anything," he said. "I heard you were being Santa and I wanted to come tell you you're a loser."

"Don't call him that!" Cindy said. She reached over and smacked Scott's forehead. He got off my lap and told her to shut up.

"You shut up," she said. "If you don't, I have a box of a hundred candy canes right here and they're all going to mysteriously disappear after I shove them up your butt." Scott grumbled something to himself, but he walked out.

"Hey, that was cool," I told Cindy. "Thanks."

"Nobody calls you a loser," she said. "Nobody."

For the most part, the kids were nice, but some tried to pull my beard off. The last kid was a little girl, about five years old. She wore a torn jacket and ripped pants. As I held her, I wondered if Nellie would have looked like her.

"What would you like for Christmas, ho, ho, ho," I said cheerfully. I sounded like the biggest idiot in the world.

"I want clothes," she said. "I've been really good this year. It's so cold outside and this jacket doesn't keep me warm anymore. Please, Santa, please?"

"Ho, ho, ho, of course," I said and gave her a candy cane and a little toy truck. "Santa has lots of clothes at the North Pole just waiting for you." I got the girl's name from her ina before they left and passed it on to the Puentes. I hoped they had some clothes to give her.

When the event was finally over, Cindy asked me if I could get her something for Christmas. I nodded and she sat in my lap.

"Can you take the beard off, Nimo? You look like a drunk wizard."

"Yeah, it's hot as hell with this thing on me," I said and tore it off. "Anyway, ho, ho, ho, what would you like?"

"Santa," she said. "I'd like a boyfriend this year."

"I'm fresh out of those, sorry," I said.

"What?" she said. "You mean I was good all year long for nothing?"

"Okay, what kind of boyfriend do you want? Maybe I can get my elves to make one for you. Tall? Handsome? Apache?"

"Nimo," Cindy said and placed her head on my chest. "I really like you. I would love to have you for Christmas."

"Oh," I said. "Me? But you can have any boy you want. And I live all the way over here and you're all the way in California."

"I don't care, Nimo. I like you."

"Guess I'll have to wrap myself up then," I said. Cindy laughed and she picked up torn wrapping paper pieces the kids left behind to wrap me up. Within minutes, I was covered in layers of wrapping paper. She even put a bow on my forehead.

"You're so beautiful," I told her.

"See Nimo?" she said. "This is why I like you."

When it was time for Cindy to go home, Ate drove her to the Rapid City Regional Airport and I sat in the backseat with her, holding her hand. I walked with her through the lobby, but soon it was time for her to board her plane.

"I guess I'll see you for the LA Pow Wow, right?" Cindy asked. "Next time I come here, I'll come during summer and you can take me to Mount Rushmore."

"Oh, it's just some big heads," I said. "You can see heads anywhere. But if that's what you want, I'll take you." I hugged her closely. I didn't want to let her go.

"Listen, I have money saved up and if I keep working enough,

I can probably go see you for Valentine's Day or Spring Break. I'll call you every day too, I promise. It's gonna be tough, but I really like you, Cindy. I think we can make this work."

"Thanks for a nice vacation, Nimo," she said and hugged me. She inched her head up to my cheek and kissed me. Then she gave me one last hug and walked away to her terminal. I watched Cindy disappear down the hallway and a tear fell from my eye.

"Goodbyes always suck, son," Ate said and rubbed my back. "You'll see her soon. I used to drive 40 miles to visit Ina on the rez and I couldn't take her out as much as I wanted to because I was so broke. I know men are supposed to be strong, but one thing that will always get to us is a pretty lady."

"LA's more than 40 miles away," I said. "I wish I could drive to her house, but I can't. If I went to Mount Rushmore and stood on Washington's head, I still wouldn't be able to see her house. This sucks."

"Nimo, you're getting older," he went on and put his arm around my shoulders. "Within a couple years or so, you're gonna fall in love the way I fell in love with Ina."

"How did you fall in love with Ina anyway?" I asked.

"Lots of reasons, son," Ate said. "She's beautiful, she's funny, she don't put up with crap, especially my crap. And I got more crap than a backed up bathroom at the Greyhound station. And she's got the greatest butt ever known to mankind."

"Ate, quit it," I said.

"Just remember one thing about dating, son," he said, clearing his throat.

"Ate, no, not the sex talk again," I groaned and slouched my shoulders. "Last time we talked about dating, all you told me was 'if you want a kid, fire in the hole. If you don't, then fire in the sock.'"

"It's a little piece of advice my tunkasila James Eagle told me a long time ago when I was first dating Ina," Ate said. "If you feel a little warmth in your heart instead of your pants, that's love."

The Departure

*A*s I fumbled with my keys to open my door when I came home from work, I felt a hand touch my shoulder. I quickly elbowed whoever it was in the stomach.

"Geez Nimo," John David groaned in pain.

"What the hell are you doing here this late?" I said. He told me to shut up and open the door. We went inside and he rushed to my room.

"Okay, what's going on?" I asked. "And it better be important, it's 2am. I had to run to work and help Mr. Black Bear fix a busted water pipe."

"I gotta stay with you for a couple days," he said. "I was over at Ignacio's. His dad walked in on us making out. Mr. Puente tried to hit me, but Ignacio threw himself in front of me and took the blows. My ina said I should stay with you until they cool off."

"You can take my bed, I'll crash on the couch," I said and grabbed an extra blanket and pillow from my closet. "How's Ignacio doing? Was he hurt?"

"Yeah," John David said. "He didn't fight back at all. I wanted to protect him, but I was really scared. He probably thinks I don't love him." John David stared at the carpet, rubbing his eyes. "I never wanted him to get hurt."

The next morning, I was up early. I drove to the rez gym to see if I could find Ignacio. I went inside and there he was, sprinting on a treadmill.

"Are you doing okay now?" I asked him. He stopped the treadmill and stuck his face close to mine, breathing heavily. There was a fresh bruise near his right eye.

"My dad beat his seal of approval into me," he said. "This wouldn't have happened if JD hadn't asked me to make out. I knew we should have never gotten together. I should have dated one of the thousand girls who asked me out."

"C'mon Ignacio," I said. "You guys couldn't keep it a secret forever. We live on Pine Ridge rez, stuff here gets around faster than germs."

"Shut up, Nimo, get the hell outta my face."

"Me? What did I do? You're obviously not as in love with John David as I thought you were," I said and turned around to walk away. He got off the treadmill, grabbed me by my shirt, and held me tight against a wall.

"Look," he said. "Last night, I took a beating so JD wouldn't have to. Don't you dare tell me I don't love him."

"Yeah, but when you love someone a lot, you don't-"

"Nimo," Ignacio said and held onto me tighter. "If you keep talking, I'm gonna rip your tongue out and shove it up your ass." He loosened his grip around me. I left before he could kill me.

By the time I got back home, John David and my parents were eating breakfast. I wanted to tell John David that Ignacio wasn't worth it right then. But I didn't talk to him about it until the middle of the day.

"I went to the gym this morning," I said. "And Ignacio almost murdered me."

"Geez Nimo, what'd you do? Give him a Playboy?"

"Hey, no offense or anything," I said and hosed down the hood of my car. "But I don't think he loves you as much as he says he does." John David grabbed the hose from me and sprayed me in the face, knocking me down to the ground. He told me I didn't know what the hell I was talking about.

"Man, when I first started going out with Cindy," I said as I heaved myself up. "I went around telling everyone about us. When you and Ignacio got together, he didn't say anything about it. He should at least stand up to his parents for you."

"You're such an idiot," John David said. "You're not in love with a man."

Even though me and John David weren't talking much, he was still living in my house after two weeks. We had finals at school and graduation was coming up. Ignacio and John David pretended they didn't know each other during the school day, but as soon as the bell rang, I'd catch them in the parking lot, holding hands between the cars. I always thought Ignacio was good for John David, but now I wasn't too sure. They looked right together and the thought of them breaking up bothered me.

A lot of people at school dated and I'd say 80 percent of those couples broke up within three months. Scott and Claudia had been together since eighth grade and Scott was the biggest asshole on Pine Ridge. There were plenty of times I saw Scott slap Claudia's butt in public or call her fat when she ate a hot dog at Big Bat's. John David and Ignacio loved each other though. I never heard either of them talk smack about each other. But they were gay and just that was too much for some people. It didn't matter they had been together longer than most other couples at school.

"Nimo," I heard Ignacio's voice say to me on the last day of school. I was standing at my locker, cleaning out my pictures of Cindy. I turned around and closed my eyes, waiting for him to hit me.

"I'm not ugly, you can look at me," he said. I opened my eyes and he hugged me so tight, he lifted me off the floor.

"Sorry for being a dick to you," he told me. "Me and JD would rather deal with this ourselves, okay? We still love each other, even if it doesn't look like it."

"Yeah, I understand," I said. "But please don't hold me against a wall again, I almost pissed myself." Ignacio promised me he wouldn't and we shook hands. His grip was tight and it hurt my hand.

After school, I went to work at Spotted Elk College. I found Mr. Black Bear and Ate fixing a water fountain near the main lobby. Ate banged on it with his wrench. He called it a son of a bitch three times.

"Ate, don't hurt its feelings," I said.

"Son, this piece of crap's been giving us trouble all afternoon," he said. "We've tried and tried and the water supply keeps leaking out. Noe, aren't you supposed to be on your break?"

"Watching you trying to fix stuff is much more entertaining," Mr. Black Bear said. "Nimo, you should have seen him earlier. We redid the white paint in the main office and your ate tripped on a loose cord and smashed his face into one of the paint cans. He looked like an ugly ghost!"

146

"Noe, take your break before I break you!" Ate said. Mr. Black Bear hurried down the hallway. Ate gave me his wrench and rubbed the sweat off his forehead with an oily towel. His rubber wedding ring was covered in rust residue and water. He made himself a rubber ring since he couldn't wear his real one at work. I hunched down next to him to try to shut the fountain's water supply off completely, but I turned the wrench too far and water spewed right into our faces.

"All right, that's it," Ate said. He got out his hammer and whacked the left side of the fountain. Water flowed down to the floor and we slipped and fell on our stomachs.

"I'm gonna rip that thing out and throw it out the window like in One Flew Over the Cuckoo's Nest!" he said. Ate and me spent twenty minutes stopping the water fountain and we wasted an hour cleaning the floor with Mr. Black Bear. After the three of us changed into some clean clothes we kept in the storage room, Ate called Ina.

"Babe," he said into his cellphone. "Your voice always fixes the crappiest days." I heard Ina say he was the cutest head facility technician she ever saw and he blushed. John David blushed the same way when Ignacio spoke to him for the first time.

"Well, I'm going home," Mr. Black Bear told me and Ate as we walked towards the main doors. "I'll see you tomorrow, Jay Eagle. See you at graduation, Nimo. I heard you got all honors or something like that."

"I did," I said. "Valedictorian, Good Citizen Award, and Best English Student Honor Award for the essays I wrote this year."

"Wow," he said. "I wish Scott had your brains. That hoksila can't even figure out how to do repair work like me."

"Not like you're any better at repair work, Noe," Ate said.

Mr. Black Bear waved goodnight to us and walked to his car across the parking lot. Ate kept on walking with me since we parked in the same area.

"You know, son," Ate said when we reached my car. "You're a good repairman. You busted a pipe today, but that's all right. One day, you might be head of facilities, but I think you got greater things going for you."

"Thanks Ate," I said and got in my car. He got into his truck and I followed him home.

By graduation day, John David was back at his house and Ignacio was living with him temporarily. I put my gown on and tucked my cap under my arm while I waited for Ate and Ina to get ready. Ina was dressed way before Ate. Ate never graduated from high school. She said he wanted to look his best. An hour later, he emerged from the master bedroom dressed in a brand new suit with his hair neatly combed.

"Wow, Ate, looking good," I said. "Did you get it at the thrift store?"

"I sure did," he said. "It was real cheap because somebody died while wearing it."

"Jay Eagle!" Ina said and pulled on his ponytail.

"Josie, you need to get some dresses people died in. We'd save a lot on the clothing bill every year. Nimo, your graduation gown was $40. When you graduate from college, you're wearing a sandwich board that says "I'm smart.""

At the ceremony, I spotted Ignacio and John David in a corner. They looked like they were fighting about something and I wanted to ask what was wrong, but I didn't want Ignacio to kill me either. Principal Eagle Bull made them get back in their seats. John David sat down with a big frown on his face.

After graduation was over, Ina asked Ate to go to Sioux Nation to get drinks for the party they were throwing for me. I went along and while we were in the juice aisle, we saw the Puentes yelling at Ignacio in Spanish. Since John David taught me some Spanish, I picked up a lot of the conversation. They told Ignacio they wanted to send him away for college so he couldn't be with John David. Ignacio didn't say a word to them.

"Hi Mrs. Puente," I butted in. "Hi Mr. Puente. How are you doing?"

"Congrats Nimo," Mr. Puente said. "If you run into your sissy friend, tell him to stay away from Ignacio."

"Antonio, maybe we should talk about this some more," Mrs. Puente told him as she rubbed his arm. Mr. Puente flinched away from her. He called John David a faggot, Sodomite, and a demonic drag queen.

"Mr. Puente," I said. "Please don't call him those things."

"Don't you tell me what to do, you're not even a Christian. What kind of wisdom would you have?"

"Antonio!" Mrs. Puente said.

"He's a really good guy, Mr. Puente," I said. "If you got to know him, I think you would like him." Ignacio tapped my shoulder. He shook his head at me. I slipped away with my fingertips in my ears.

A couple weeks went by and John David and Ignacio only talked to each other past midnight over the phone. But when July rolled around, John David showed up at my house at one in the morning with a black eye.

"What the hell happened to you?" I said and shoved him inside. He told me he snuck into Ignacio's room and Mr. Puente caught them hugging each other. On top of that,

Ignacio broke up with him for good.

"What an asshole," I said. "Let's get him, John David."

"Tomorrow," he said and lowered himself down on the couch. "I don't wanna talk about him right now." He held his hand over his eye and fell asleep right away.

In the morning, John David and me went to the Temple of God's Love on Sundance Road. We found Ignacio at the front desk. He was so busy typing away at the computer, he didn't notice John David standing over him.

"I told you to stay away from me," Ignacio said. "We're done, JD. Get over it."

"I'm not getting over jack shit," John David said. "It's not my fault your parents hate us being together. Why don't you stand up to them?"

"Because I told them I'm not gay," Ignacio said. "It's just a phase."

"Ignacio, you are so gay, you can't even think straight," John David said. I laughed and Ignacio glared at me.

"Stop saying that, we're in church for God's sake," Ignacio said and got up from the desk. He walked towards the chapel and John David trailed behind him.

"You never acted straight when we were alone together," John David said.

"JD, please," Ignacio said as he opened the chapel doors.

"Why don't you tell them about how we had sex on our first date?" John David said. "And what about the time when you said you wanted to marry me someday? Remember? You told me you wanted to elope to a state where it's legal."

"JD, go home," Ignacio said. "You'll get both of us in trouble if you don't shut up." But John David followed him into the chapel and I went after them. Mr. Puente was at the podium, in the middle of a sermon. We sat down in the very back row. John David kept trying to talk to Ignacio. He didn't notice the church members staring at him. One woman looked at him with her tongue sticking out. I tried to tell John David we should leave, but he wouldn't budge away from Ignacio.

"I love you," he whispered to him. "I don't want anyone else."

"John David, please," Ignacio said. Mr. Puente finished his sermon. Then he started praising God for Ignacio 'not being a Sodomite after all.' Almost the whole congregation clapped and cheered. I saw a few people shaking their heads. The woman who stuck her tongue at John David stood up and she slammed her hands together, trying to clap the loudest. John David jumped on top of the pew with his mouth wide open.

"The hell he isn't!" John David yelled. Everyone turned to look at him and I told him to shut up. He already had one black eye – he didn't need another one.

"JD, if you don't shut up right now, I'm gonna beat your mouth off your face," Ignacio said. But John David ran up to Mr. Puente at the podium and said "Ignacio Puente is gay" into the microphone. Mr. Puente snatched the microphone from him.

"My boy isn't a Sodomite," Mr. Puente said. "He's a good, decent, Christian boy. As for you, you're nothing but an anal sex lover." John David took the microphone from Mr. Puente again and said "I have had sex with Ignacio Puente many, many times. If you don't believe me, he has a birthmark on his right butt cheek and it looks exactly like a rocket ship." Ignacio covered his face with his hands. The whole audience was quiet.

John David and Ignacio didn't talk to each other for three

weeks after the church incident. Surprisingly, Ignacio wasn't mad about it. He even showed up at Hunting Grounds, the little coffee shop across the street from Big Bat's where John David was a barista. I sat at the counter, sipping on an iced hot chocolate, watching Ignacio apologize to John David at the register. While he did, John David called him a 'hetero' and it wasn't in the playful way he would call me 'hetero.'

"You say you love me and you can't even tell your parents about me," John David told him. "Get lost, Ignacio."

About a week later, I met up with Ignacio at Big Bat's for lunch. I tried to get John David to come with me, but he told me he would rather eat his own balls with barbecue sauce than eat lunch with Ignacio. Ignacio came to Big Bat's with a black Oakland Raiders cap on. He had the brim tilted down over his right eye to cover the scar Mr. Puente gave him.

"John David misses you," I said. "He might say he wants to gouge your eyes out with a pitchfork and hang your dead body up on Mount Rushmore, but he misses you."

"I've done everything I can," Ignacio said. "I called him, I went to his house, I went to his job, I wrote him a letter, I left a note on his truck, and it's useless."

"John David loves you a lot. He'll calm down soon."

"I dunno, Nimo. For the past couple days, I've been driving home after work in tears. Some church members say they want to kill homosexuals and they don't know I'm one and I love one. My dad thinks I'm just acting weird and I'll like women eventually."

"He can't say that forever," I said. "I mean, you love John David, right?"

"Of course I do," he said. "But maybe we aren't meant for each other."

"You know, Ignacio," I began. "Sometimes, when you love someone, you have to just let family be family. My unci didn't like my ate and she really got mad when he proposed to my ina. But they got married anyway because they wanted to. If your parents see how much you love John David, I think everything will work out."

"It's not easy," he said. "I really wish I wasn't gay and John David was a girl or the other way around. Everything would be so much better." Ignacio ate the last of his hot dog and told me he'd see me around.

For a while, I didn't see or hear from Ignacio at all. I asked John David if he did and told me "Good riddance," but he looked worried about him. We figured Ignacio was working a lot or staying indoors to avoid embarrassment, especially since people started calling him 'Rocket Ship Butt Cheek' wherever he went. Soon, it was over a month since we last saw him and our classes at Spotted Elk College already started. It wasn't natural to disappear from the rez the way Ignacio did. No matter how big the rez was, people always kept track of each other. On a Sunday afternoon, Ina and me stopped by the Puente house to see what was up.

"Ignacio's fine, he's at school," Mrs. Puente said.

"But it's Sunday, the college is closed," I said. Mr. Puente told me Ignacio was at school – San Francisco State University.

"JD's gonna be devastated," Ina said during our drive home. "I was so happy when he met Ignacio. He had the very same look on his face I did when I met your ate."

"Ina, John David will be all right, he's tough," I said, but she didn't hear me. Ate sat on the porch, carving a pipe, and sweating all over.

"Jay Eagle, you really need a shower," Ina told him. "The presidents at Mount Rushmore can smell you from here."

"Geez Josie, didn't our vows say something about for better or for worse?"

"They didn't say nothing about me staying with you if you stink," Ina said and put her arms around his neck.

For a couple of days, I didn't mention Ignacio to John David. One night after class, we ate some burgers at Big Bat's and he said, "Nimo, I wish Ignacio was here with us right now. I miss him."

"He, uh, can't hang out with us anymore," I said and stuffed a couple of French fries in my mouth. John David asked what was wrong with him. I swallowed my fries and took a long drink of my soda.

"He's," I said. "He's gone."

"He's dead? When the hell did that happen, Nimo? Why didn't you tell me about this? Damn, I shouldn't have been such an ass when he tried to talk to me."

"He's not dead, his parents sent him to San Francisco State," I said. John David pushed his half-eaten burger aside.

"You mean he left me?"

"Hey," I shrugged. "Maybe it was a last minute thing. He can't stay in San Francisco forever. He might not like it there."

"Nimo, what kind of gay man wouldn't like San Francisco?"

"Well," I said. "Maybe he's the one gay dude in the whole world who won't like it there. Wanna head home?" He only nodded.

We got in my car and I drove to his house. John David sat really close to the passenger door, looking out the window and not saying a word. He waved goodnight to me and headed towards his front door. When I put my car into reverse, I saw John David sit on his porch steps. He pulled his shirt over his eyes.

Lost Angeles

*M*y parents might have had money troubles my whole life, but they always somehow saved up enough for us to visit the annual Los Angeles Pow Wow. They would sell their crafts and I'd grass dance. But one year, I didn't dance. My parents left for the pow wow early in the morning and I told them I'd be on my way later since I wanted to visit Cindy first. I caught the #4 bus from our hotel and got off on Vine Street, two blocks away from her place. After I passed by the Hollywood Forever Cemetery, a red car with a purple driver's door swerved onto the sidewalk.

I woke up in the ER with my parents hugging me and praying in Lakota. A piece of metal from the car sliced through my leg. I spent 18 days in the hospital and missed my flight home. Ina went home a week after I was released. Sioux Nation needed her back so much, they paid her flight change fee. I stayed behind with Ate at the Presidential Suites of Inglewood, a small hotel owned by Harry Iron Horse. We met Harry at the LA Pow Wow years before and he let Ate and me stay there for free. The day after Ina left, Ate was still asleep, clutching his wallet-sized picture of Ina in his hand.

"Ahhhtay," I said as I nudged him.

"Lemme sleep, Josie, I'm tired."

"I'm not Ina, she went home."

"That's right," Ate yawned. "I miss my babe too much." He hopped up to his feet, rubbing his eyes.

"What are we doing today, Ate?"

"Hollywood," he said. "Those tourists loved our feathers."

"Ate, I can't take any more pictures with tourists, I'm not a landmark."

"That don't matter when we gotta pay all your medical bills and get plane tickets to go home. Put your feathers on, Geronimo Jay Thunderclap. It's either taking pictures with tourists or doing it with old, rich dudes in Beverly Hills. At least the feathers don't require touching a wrinkly ass." I sunk my head and threw my feathers into my backpack.

Three bus rides later, we stood by Barbra Streisand's star on the Walk of Fame dressed in our regalia. Tourists flocked to us for pictures. We made $80 in half an hour. When we were close to making $100, an elderly woman jumped in front of our eager customer and told him to leave.

"Native Americans believe taking pictures of them robs their soul," she told our customer. "You are being disrespectful towards our people."

"Our people?" Ate said.

"Yes sir," the elderly woman nodded. "I'm 1/80th Cherokee. What tribe are you?"

"My son and I are proud members of the you-ain't-Cherokee-go-away tribe," he said. We made close to $500 by the end of the afternoon and then we walked a couple blocks down the street to Mel's for hamburgers.

"Ate, do we really believe taking pictures robs our soul?" I asked as he rubbed excess grease from his chin.

"Not if someone's paying us."

"We made a lot of dough today, didn't we?"

"We did," he said with a laugh. "We keep this up, we can get home next month."

"Leksi said he'd wire us some money."

"He can keep his money," Ate said and took a long gulp of his lemonade. "Your ina's back home, she's gonna work hard and save up some money for us. I don't let no one pay for my problems except myself, your ina, or the US government."

"You hate the US government, Ate."

"I'm Lakota, Nimo, I got plenty of reasons to hate the US government," Ate said. "Especially after what they did to the sacred Black Hills. One of these days, I'm gonna sneak up there and carve my ass into the hill across from the heads. I'll call it Mount Assmore. Better yet, I'll call it Mount Sequoia Red Cloud after your unci." I put my burger down and covered my laughs with my hands.

Normally, I would have loved being stuck in Los Angeles. I wasn't because Cindy and I weren't a couple anymore. We were together for three years and despite us being long distance, I really thought we would get married someday. When Cindy turned 18, her dad helped her get her apartment as a gift for getting into UCLA. I also got into UCLA, so Cindy and I were planning to live together until she met Alan Redhawk at work. Six months later, he was living where I was supposed to live.

The next morning, I took a bus to the apartment Cindy shared with Alan. As I walked the remaining blocks, I tripped over a sleeping homeless guy and fell on my face. I brushed the dirt off myself, fixed my ponytail, and walked the last block to Cindy's apartment, hoping I still looked good enough.

"Nimo!" Cindy said when she answered the door. She gave me a big hug and asked how my leg was doing. I pretended to be in pain so I could have an excuse to slouch down to her sweet face.

"How's your progress on getting back to Pine Ridge?"

"Me and my dad are working to get some cash."

"I'm sorry about your accident," she said. "You never told me how it happened."

"It was a little past Hollywood Forever Cemetery."

"What? What were you doing all the way over here?"

"Oh, I wanted to stop by Astro Burger before going to the pow wow," I said. She didn't have to know the truth.

Cindy gave me another tight hug. Her hair shined and her lazy eye seemed to be little more open than it ever was. I looked to my right. There was a framed photo of Cindy and Alan over the fireplace. They were on the Ferris wheel at the Santa Monica Pier. I knew because that's exactly where I took her for a date when we first got together.

"If you stay a little longer, Alan can give you a ride to your hotel," Cindy said. I told Cindy I was okay with taking the bus and went towards her door. She tapped my bad leg and kissed my knee. My leg was sore from all the walking I did earlier. It hurt like hell to have it touched, but it was the best pain I've ever felt.

A couple days later, Cindy asked if I could meet her in Santa Monica for dinner. I took the wrong bus and ended up in a rough neighborhood. Two morons jumped on me and tried to grab my wallet. I reached in my pocket for Ate's carving knife.

"I'm gonna castrate the both of you," I said and took out the knife. They let me keep my cash but they also threw me against the wall and I crashed into a trashcan. I brushed the dirt from myself and got on the next bus to Santa Monica.

An hour later, I met up with Cindy and jerkoff, I mean Alan, at Greens Up, Cindy's favorite restaurant. During dinner, Alan held Cindy's hand and looked me in the eyes. He started full on making out with her, but she pushed him away.

"Alan, we're out in public," she said. Alan didn't care. He kissed her multiple times on her mouth and ran his hand on her cheek, the way I used to do.

"Baby, stop it," Cindy said. Alan finally let go of her. I dropped my fork and quickly stabbed my bad leg under the table to make myself squeal.

"Are you okay?" Cindy asked me. She hunched down to look at my leg, but Alan pulled her back and shoved his damn tongue in her mouth again.

"I need to go, my leg's acting up," I said and got up from my chair.

"Alan sweetie, can you give him a ride home?"

"I guess so," he said, rolling up his sleeves and showing off his muscular arms. He stood up from his chair, rubbing his toned abdomen.

"It's okay," I said. "I can take the bus."

When I got back to Presidential Suites, I found Ate on the bed with a basket of French fries, chicken wings, and a large iced tea on the nightstand next to him. Roseanne blared on the television. He laughed hard at the episode.

"Ate, you know you're not supposed to eat this stuff."

"I'm enjoying it now before we get home and your ina makes me cauliflower soup again. What the hell happened to you?

You're all dirty."

"I got jumped," I said. "And thrown against a trashcan. And stabbed with a fork."

"Every time you go after Cindy, you get hurt. You should take it as a sign."

"I have a sign, I'm ugly," I said.

"No you ain't, son," he said. "I take that as an insult."

"I didn't call you ugly, Ate."

"The hell you didn't. I made you and I don't think I'm ugly. And Ina made you too and if you even think Ina's ugly, I'll ground you from now until your midlife crisis. Anyway, son, you need to get a new girl. Ask her out on April Fool's Day. If she says no, you can say you were joking."

"Ate, c'mon."

"Listen up, hoksila," he said. "If Cindy really wanted to be with you, you'd be living in her apartment right now. It don't matter if you live on Pine Ridge and she's down here in Hollyweird. She would have found a way. Screw her, Nimo. Screw her."

"What if Ina wanted to break up with you?"

"She won't," he said. "She needs me to fix the doorbell when we get home."

At the end of the month, the LAPD still hadn't found the person who ran me over, but my medical bills were paid off thanks to Ina, Leksi and Tunwinla, the tourists at the Walk of Fame, and some people on Pine Ridge who donated. However, the airline refused to waive our flight change fees unless I had a valid emergency to go home. So, Dad had an idea. We took a bus to Mr. Blackbird's print shop in Culver City. Ate wanted him to create a fake doctor's note saying I needed to go back to South Dakota for an emergency surgery on my leg.

"Both of us could get in a lotta trouble for that," Mr. Black-bird said. "And why wouldn't Geronimo be able to have emergency surgery here?"

"Because we're Lakota and we believe having surgery in California robs our souls. C'mon, Vermont. I'll give you $50," Ate told him. Ate called Mr. Blackbird 'Vermont' because he thinks he looks like the state of Vermont when he stands sideways.

"Jay Eagle, why do you call me Vermont?"

"You grew up on Vermont Avenue, didn't you?"

"You grew up on Rosebud rez and I don't call you Rosebud."

"Are you gonna do us the favor or what, Vermont?" Ate said. Vermont, I mean, Mr. Blackbird, really didn't want to get involved and sent us on our way. Ate suggested we put on our regalia and head to Hollywood for the billionth time.

"I wanna go home, Nimo," Ate said. "City of Angels, my ass. If this was the city of angels, I could get a pair of wings and fly home to your ina." Ate looked at his wedding ring. He rubbed it between his fingers slowly.

Instead of going to Hollywood to bother more tourists, Ate and me went back to the hotel. After he fell asleep while watching All in the Family, I called Mr. Blackbird.

"Geronimo, I already told your dad I'm not gonna do that."

"Mr. Blackbird," I said. "I still love your daughter."

"No you don't," he said, almost laughing. "She's engaged and she lives with Alan. How could you still love her, wait a minute, do you?"

"I never stopped loving her."

"Oh Geronimo," he responded. "I always thought you were a nice guy for her. I can't stand Alan. He always comes in my shop with his hands all over her like she's a walking steak. I'll see what I can do for you."

"Thanks. I wanted to tell you this earlier, but my dad hates it when I talk about her, after all that happened, you know."

"Geronimo, love is tricky," he said. "Cindy's mother and I divorced almost ten years ago. She cheated on me more times than I can count. I don't hate her. I should, but I don't. Maybe I'm an idiot. I'll pay your fees, don't worry about it. Get yourself home."

"Are you sure? That's 600 bucks."

"Well, you love Cindy. Any guy who loves my daughter as much as you do is fine by me. Is there any way I could send Alan to Pine Ridge and keep you here?"

"I wish. If Cindy wasn't engaged, I'd stay."

"You're a nice kid. I wish you were the guy marrying Cindy. By this time next year, I'll be related to an asshole."

A week later, Ate and me took bus #3 from Inglewood to LAX Airport five hours before our flight. He wore his best clothes and even got a haircut.

"Gotta look good for your ina," he said. "When we get home, I want her to look at me and fall in love all over again."

"I'm sure she'd be okay with you wearing a garbage bag, Ate."

"You'd think. She likes me wearing nice clothes. As for her, she can wear a ripped up, used garbage bag and still look hotter than the sun."

Cindy told me she'd meet me at the airport to say goodbye. When she finally got to LAX, I was 30 minutes away from boarding time. She said she was going to take the bus, but Alan doesn't like her riding alone, so she waited all morning for him. As the douchebag drove around the airport, we walked past the platforms and into a secluded area. I looked at my watch, seeing I had about 15 minutes left.

"I gotta go," I frowned.

"Are you coming back next year?" she asked.

"I don't know," I said. She looked at me with her soft brown eyes and kissed my forehead. A second later, we were making out. I hadn't kissed her in a long time and forgot how much I enjoyed it. I wanted to tell her to dump Alan and then ditch my flight to South Dakota, but I didn't.

"You're still a good kisser," she winked.

"So are you," I said. We walked back out to the platform to wait for Alan to show up. I gave Cindy a final hug when Alan pulled up to the curb.

"Bye Nimo!" she called out and slid into Alan's car. I was about to wave at them but my bad leg twisted and I fell on the platform. As I stood up, I saw Alan's red car very close. His purple driver door shined under the sunlight.

"Geronimo Jay Thunderclap!" Ate shouted over the airport traffic. "I already missed this flight once, I ain't missing it again!" I tried to talk to him, but he grabbed my arm and pulled me to Gate 67. Once we were seated on the plane, Ate rubbed his wedding ring and pulled down the shade of the window on his right.

"I don't wanna see this damn place for a long time," he said. "Hollyweird, Walk of Shame, Beverly Hills of Crap, City of Coked Up Angels."

"Sir, that's no way to speak of my home city," a lady behind us said.

"Ma'am, I'm from South Dakota," Ate answered. "And in South Dakota, we don't give a shit about what people think, especially you. The heads on Mount Rushmore got more brains than you and they're made out of rocks."

164

"You are the rudest man I've ever seen in my life!"

"Ma'am," I said. "Don't mind him. He just wants to go home, like me."

When I got back to Pine Ridge, it was hard to adjust. It felt weird to not see the Hollywood sign every day, but stray dogs, Ray Firebird jumping at cars, and kids playing basketball. The day after I got home, the first thing I did was pick up John David, drive to Big Bat's, fill up my car with gas, and order two hot dogs with chips and a lemon slushy. While I was there, I saw Scott try to make out with Claudia and she hit him with a frying pan. Mr. Graywolf laughed really loud and Mrs. Graywolf did too. The other customers high fived me when they saw me inside.

"I'm so glad you're back, Nimo," John David as we ate. "It was so boring here without you. The other night I was so bored, I helped my mom clip coupons and organize them by expiration date. Did you hear Scott and Claudia broke up? He keeps trying to get her back and she keeps saying no."

"Why? What happened?"

"Claudia's doing real well at Spotted Elk College and Scott flunked out. He told her to flunk out too and she told him no way."

"Really? I guess that's better for her. I was wondering when she would get tired of dating toilet paper. Hey, since I'm single and she's single, maybe I'll ask her out."

"I'm gonna ask out Scott just to piss him off," John David said. "So what's gonna happen with Alan? Did you tell the cops?"

"I did, they asked me if I want to press charges, but since I'm all right, I said no."

"You said no? He could've killed you!"

"Yeah, but then I'd have to go to court in LA and I do not wanna go back there. Cindy broke up with him, I think that's enough for me."

"Whoa!" he said, as if I was talking about a celebrity. "She broke up with him? Man, this is a bad year for jerk boyfriends."

"She called me to tell me she broke up with him," I said. "She didn't say anything about getting back together with me, so it's over between us. My ate's right. If she really loved me, she wouldn't have dumped me right before I moved over there. But, before I left, I got to make out with her one last time. That was awesome."

"He is right, you deserve the best," John David said and sipped on his slushy. "You'll meet a nice girl one day, Nimo. You'll meet her when you're not even looking."

When I got home, I heard Ina and Ate giggling in the kitchen. Ina was dividing her time between frying chicken strips and kissing Ate. She turned one strip over, kissed him, ran back to the stove to turn another, and kissed him again. It was a game they played on occasion. Basically, Ina had to give Ate a kiss for each year of their marriage without burning any of the chicken strips. If she won, Ate had to do the dishes after dinner for three days in a row. When it came to that game, Ate always lost miserably.

"I win again!" Ina said.

"Aw Josie, I suck at this game," Ate groaned. "Can we do another round?"

"No, Jay Eagle, you lose, you do the dishes," Ina said. They hugged and shared a couple of post-game kisses. Ate lifted Ina from the floor to kiss her even closer, as he always does after their game. Ina giggled as he held her.

"I missed you so much," she told him. "You wouldn't believe how many men I killed while I waited for you. I got rid of the corpses the day before you came home."

"I believe you," Ate said. "If I loved you the first day I saw you, why wouldn't any other guy feel the same? You are smoking hot, Josie, I just wanna-"

"Are you two done? I'm gonna puke if you're not," I said.

"Nimo! You're home!" Ina said when she spotted me.

"Yeah, I'm home," I said. "I'm home, finally."

The Fork

For my 22nd birthday, John David got me tickets for The Mars Spiders, a David Bowie cover band. They were going to perform at Rushmore Live in Rapid City. On Friday afternoon, we headed out for a weekend trip.

Right when we got to Rapid City, we stopped at a gas station. John David stayed outside to smoke. I went inside and browsed the drink aisles. As I stood in the register line, I looked out the window and I saw three guys holding John David down on the pavement. They were punching his face, kicking his body, and yelling "faggot." I dropped the drinks on the floor and ran out, but by then, the guys took off in their car. John David was face down on the ground with his pants off and a carving fork lodged in his butt. He was bleeding all over, especially from a gash on his lower back. I didn't see the guys too well, but I knew they were from Pine Ridge. Nobody can tell John David is gay just by looking at him.

"John David," I said and shook him by his shoulder after I called 911. "John David, wake up. They're gone now. Wake up, man." He didn't. When the paramedics finally arrived, John

David was still unconscious. They strapped him on a stretcher and wheeled him inside the ambulance. A cop showed up soon after to question me.

"What happened? Who did this guy in?" he asked.

"Three guys with ponytails."

"What'd they look like?"

"Indians," I said and watched the ambulance take John David away.

"C'mon guy, you ain't helping," he said.

"They looked like me," I said and showed him my own ponytail. "I didn't see them too good, but I know they had ponytails."

"Are you telling me three clones of yourself beat up your friend?"

"Actually, yeah," I frowned. He took my name down and left.

I got in my car, looked at the clock, and saw I had enough time to get to the concert but I took a U-turn towards the hospital. When I got there, a nurse escorted me to the waiting room. The old TV was playing an episode of All in the Family but I couldn't focus. I stepped out into the hallway to call home.

"They stuck a carving fork in his butt," I said to Ina. "A fork!"

"How awful, Nimo," she said. "Do you want me and Ate to go up there?"

"Nah, I don't think you two wanna drive out here," I answered. To be honest, I did want them to come. I wanted a hug from Ina and a dirty joke from Ate.

"If you say so," Ina said. "Keep John David comfortable. If somebody tries to stick another fork in him, you pray to the Creator that he gets instant diarrhea."

I went back to my car to find something to read since the

waiting room had nothing but magazines with pictures of expensive clothes. I got lucky and found a Playboy John David gave me for Christmas. I slipped one of the boring magazines over my Playboy and tried to enjoy the issue. But I kept thinking about John David. He was always a target before, but it was never violent. The worst he ever got was name calling and even then, it was usually something dumb like "fruitcake" or "fairy godmother." I couldn't get his gash out of my head.

"He's still being monitored by the doctors," the nurse told me when I asked about John David's condition. "As soon as he regains consciousness, you can go to his room. Are you his boyfriend? I can let you stay in his room overnight."

"I sure am," I said. The people around me gave me nasty looks after they heard I was 'gay.' For the first time, I knew how John David felt when people glared at him.

John David was awake sooner than I thought he would be. His chest was plastered with bandages. There was a tray of chicken, mashed potatoes, and chocolate pudding next to him, but he hadn't touched any of it. He was slouched on the bed, watching Seinfeld, but not looking interested even though it's his favorite show.

"Nimo, did the cops take the fork?" he asked me with pauses.

"Yeah, for evidence."

"Well that sucks," he said. "Now I can't eat the food the nurse brought for me." I laughed, but he kept his eyes on the television. I lounged back in the chair next to him.

"You missed the concert," John David said after a while of silence.

"Don't sweat it, I'm sure they'll have more shows later. By the way, I told the nurse I'm your boyfriend so she'd let me stay in this room with you." John David laughed, but not too hard.

"I gotta pee," John David said with a groan. "Can you help me up?"

"Aren't you supposed to use a pan?"

"Please don't talk about kitchen stuff right now, Nimo." I helped him get down from his bed and he had thick bandages with dried bloodstains on his lower back. Despite his muscular build, he felt so light while I carried him. The bandage over his gash came loose and I saw 'FAG' carved into his skin. I quickly put it back in place.

"Thanks," John David said when we reached the bathroom. "I'll take over now."

"Are you sure?" I asked. He didn't look like he could.

"Yeah, I got it under control," he said. He locked himself inside the bathroom and I heard him crying, but he probably thought I couldn't. Most of all, I hoped his bandage would stay on and he wouldn't see what was scratched into him.

"Nothing like a good long pee," John David said when he was done. I carried him back into the bed and he was knocked out right away.

John David was released from the hospital on Sunday morning. After having breakfast at a diner, we hit the road. Every time we were in my car, John David controlled the music. This time, he didn't touch the radio.

"All right, I'm putting on Madonna," I said.

"I hate her," he said. "She's seen more hot dogs than Nathan's in Coney Island, more than I'll ever see in my life." When I laughed, John David didn't respond. He set his head against the window and closed his eyes.

"Hey, I gotta take a leak," I said when we were halfway home. I pulled over to a gas station which also happened to be selling 'Indian crafts.'

"What kind of Indian is that?" I said and pointed to a carved figure of a 'chief.'

"Oh, if I had a nickel for every time I heard that," John David sighed. We went inside and headed to the restrooms. While I fixed my ponytail, I saw John David struggling to button his pants. I walked over to help him, but he almost fell backwards.

"Nimo, for the Creator's sake, someone could walk in on us."

"We're boyfriends until we get home, this could be our last chance to get busy," I said. He finally laughed, even though it still wasn't much.

When we got to Pine Ridge, it was lunchtime. John David asked to stop at my house for a drink. I saw Ate fixing crooked shingles on the roof and waved to him.

"Hi son," Ate said when we got to the porch. "Hey JD, how you doing?"

"Okay," he shrugged. He walked past me and into the house. Ate looked down at me from his ladder with a confused face.

"Some guys put a carving fork in his-"

"Right, your ina told me," Ate said. "Poor kid. I can't believe it."

"I wish I could've done something, Ate. I'm so useless."

"Don't dwell on it, Nimo, I'm sure you would've done something if you could've," Ate told me. "Glad to have you and JD home in one piece."

I walked into the living room and John David was on the couch, sipping on Hi-C, and watching Seinfeld. It was his favorite episode, the one when Jerry and Kramer take revenge on a laundromat owner. I expected him to be laughing within a couple of minutes. But it didn't happen. After the episode was over, I shut the TV off and told John David I was taking him home.

My new schedule at Spotted Elk College was from six in the morning until one in the afternoon so I could go to class and be home by dinnertime. John David always came in an hour before I got off my shift and we would head to class together. On Monday, he came in thirty minutes later than usual.

"There was a leak in the bathroom."

"Again?" I groaned.

"Well not anymore, I just finished peeing," he said. I shook my head and told him I'd meet him in class later. He walked slowly from soreness. After being hit with Alan's car in Los Angeles, my leg never fully recovered and I was left with an occasional limp. If my leg hadn't been acting up in Rapid City, I could've gotten to John David faster. Maybe I could've stopped the fork.

After my last class ended, I met up with John David at Big Bat's for dinner. The customers inside looked at John David funny. A few of them whispered to each other. I overheard some of what they said.

"I always knew someone was gonna get that hoksila," a man said to another. "Maybe he needed a beating to convince him liking boys ain't right."

"Poor child," an older woman said to Mrs. Graywolf. "His mother must be so heartbroken. I know I would be if my grandson liked arrowheads."

While we waited for our orders, John David leaned in close to me and said, "I know who did it, but it's better if we drop it. I don't want them getting you."

"What if I'm gay and I don't know it?"

"Nimo," John David said with a laugh. "You're not gay."

"I could be," I said. "I listen to a lot of Madonna."

"But," he went on. "Did you like having sex with Cindy?"

"What? We broke up a long time ago, don't bring up ancient history."

"Did you like having sex with her?"

"Yes," I frowned. He pointed and laughed at me, calling me a 'hetero.'

"Hey, it's not my fault I like girls, I was born this way."

"You know what, Nimo? I love that you're a hetero," John David said. "You don't hog up the men."

"And I love that you're not a hetero, it means more women for me," I said. John David smiled and thanked me.

On Friday night, I woke up from a post-work nap and freshened up for my latest date. Her name was Lena Buffalohead. She was John David's neighbor who recently broke up with her asshole boyfriend, Ted Elkhorn, one of Scott's buddies. I took an extra long shower and even shaved my armpits. It was our fifth date and things were going well. I came out of the bathroom in my best button down shirt and khakis.

"You look so cute, Nimo," Ina said from the couch. She was cuddling with Ate.

"He's not cute, he's not a kitten," Ate said.

"Then you're not cute either, you weirdo," Ina said. "Have a nice night, Nimo."

"And remember what I've always told you," Ate said. "If you-"

"Feel a little warmth in your heart instead of your pants, that's love," I said.

I got to Lena's with five minutes to spare. Mr. Buffalohead

answered the door before I knocked. He's known as "On Time Tom" because he's always on the dot. Some people say Mr. Buffalohead had the doctors at the Indian Health Service Hospital induce Lena's birth since he thought she would be born past her due date.

"Nimo!" Lena said when she saw me. She hugged me and kissed my cheek.

"Where you taking our little girl tonight?" Mrs. Buffalohead asked me.

"We're going to Big Bat's for dinner," I said. "And maybe to Hunting Grounds for some coffee afterwards, whatever the lady wants."

"You bring my daughter back at midnight sharp or else," Mr. Buffalohead said. "If you don't, you'll end up as the meat in a Big Bat's hamburger." Lena told her parents not to worry and we were off.

During the drive to Big Bat's, Lena held my hand and twiddled with my thumb. Lena and me took some classes together at Spotted Elk College, but I never paid attention to her since she was Ted's girlfriend. A couple weeks earlier, she stood up for John David when he was bullied by some guys while he bought cigarettes at Sioux Nation. Lena told them, "All of you need to go home and play with your joysticks."

At Big Bat's, Lena held my hand as we waited for our food. She rubbed her cheek on my upper arm and gazed into my eyes. She had a birthmark on the edge of her forehead, I'm assuming from being induced, and it looked like a jellybean. It made her face cuter than it already was.

"I really like spending time with you, Nimo," she said. "You're so sweet. I can't believe Claudia turned you down."

"Guess I have to be like Scott," I said. Lena's face got queasy.

175

"He's such an idiot," she said. "I like Claudia, but I almost never hung out with her because he'd be with her. I'm so glad they're done now."

When I finished my hot dog and fries, John David came in. He spoke in Spanish, saying he came to buy spray paint but he'd be leaving soon to give me and Lena privacy.

"He's such a nice neighbor," Lena said after John David left. "Did you know he once baked my ina some cookies when she was sick? Isn't that sweet?"

"Him or the cookies?" I asked. She smiled and fiddled with my hand some more.

"Would you mind parking somewhere with me?" she whispered.

"As long as it's not a tow-away zone," I said. Lena took my hand in hers and we went to my car.

For the first few minutes, I drove around aimlessly because I couldn't think of a good place to go. I was also pretty nervous since I hadn't kissed a girl in a while. Eventually, I parked in my usual spot at Spotted Elk College. Lena snuggled against my right arm. I reclined our seats and she kissed me first. I kissed the tip of her nose, her lips, and her neck. Lena moved closer towards me, but then she pulled herself away.

"What's wrong? Is it midnight already?" I asked.

"I thought I heard somebody screaming," she said.

"Maybe someone saw Ray Firebird naked," I said and tried to kiss her again.

"Shush, Nimo," Lena said. After a few seconds, I did hear the scream. I turned my car on and sped towards it.

I found John David a block away. Three guys held him on the ground, throwing punches at his back. They kicked him, hit his head with a tree branch, and chanted "Dirty queer." I rolled up my sleeves and puffed my chest out.

"Leave my boyfriend alone!" I shouted as loud as I could. Lena was behind me, asking me what I was talking about, but I didn't answer her.

"Gabe?" Lena said. I got a closer look and saw one of the guys was Gabe 'Angel' Buffalohead, Lena's cousin who just moved to Pine Ridge from Nebraska. Gabe didn't live up to his nickname, so I heard. The other two guys were Ted, Lena's ex, and the lovely Scott Black Bear.

"Nimo, I got it under control," John David said.

"Quiet honey, let me talk to these guys," I said. I told them to step away from him, but they laughed. They said they knew I wasn't gay and to mind my own business.

"What do you mean I'm not gay?" I said, like they had insulted me.

"Nimo," John David pleaded. Gabe laughed at me again, but I warned him to let my boyfriend go or things would get ugly.

"Nimo, you ain't a queer," Scott said. "Your best friend is, but you're more straight faced than Mount Rushmore."

"Yeah," Ted said. "You're dating my ex girl. Step off and pretend you didn't see nothing." Lena tugged at my shirt. She looked scared, but John David looked terrified.

"I'm gay," I said. "Me and John David are lovers. Right, John David?"

"You need to shut the hell up before you get us both killed," he said to me in Spanish. Ted, Scott, and Gabe laughed out loud.

"Okay, if you're really gay, kiss him," Gabe said. "On the mouth!" I said I would. They let John David stand up and walk over to me.

"You idiot, they'll stick a fork in you," he whispered in

Spanish.

"Pretend I'm Ignacio," I said.

"Nimo!" he said. "Don't be so stupid!" Before he could say more, I took him in my arms, closed my eyes, and kissed him like he was a 1980s Madonna. We kissed for a good while, enough for our tongues to join several times. When the kiss was over, I knew John David and everybody else was right – I wasn't gay.

"Geez Nimo, you turned me hetero for five seconds," John David said and spit to his left side. Gabe, Scott, and Ted looked at us with their mouths wide open. Lena was asking me what the hell was going on and I couldn't come up with a straight answer, I mean a good one. Scott lurched over and punched me twice in my stomach.

"Disgusting fag," Scott said. "Just like JD." I kicked his right leg, knocked him over, and punched him in the head. With John David's help, I fought all three of them. They were stronger than I thought, but they took off when I made Gabe's nose bleed. John David had cuts and bruises on his arms and legs. My lip was busted and pouring blood on my chin.

"Here," John David said and gave me his handkerchief. "I'll take Lena home. You've had a rough night. I'll see you later."

"Toksa Lena," I said and waved to her with blood streaming down to my shirt. She hesitated to wave back at first, but she did eventually.

I didn't get home until past midnight and lucky for me, Leksi Gray Mountain was sleeping over at our house. He got out his medicine bag and stitched me up.

"Hoksila, I didn't know you were into boxing," he said as he finished. "You'll be okay. No more fights for a while, okay?"

"I promise," I said. "I didn't mean to fight though, it kinda just happened." Ina and Ate came out from their bedroom. They both gasped.

"What happened on your date?" Ina asked.

"You'll find out by tomorrow, Ina."

"Looks like someone made out too much," Ate said with a wink.

"Uhm, not really," I said. "It was from something else."

"What?" Ate said and waved his fist in my face. "Did you try to fire in the hole when Lena didn't want you to?"

"No!" I said. "Of course not!" I was too out of it to do any more explaining. I said goodnight to everyone and hit the sack.

John David was outside my house the next morning. He had swollen bruises all over his arms. I told him I could drive him to Sioux Plains and have my leksi look at him.

"I'll be okay," he said. "Your lip's looking better."

"Thanks," I said. "But it's gonna be a while before we kiss again, it hurts a lot."

"Rumors are already spreading about you," he said and sat on my porch step. "Some don't believe it. Some say they knew it all along."

"They can say what they want, I know what's true," I said. "I don't think Lena's gonna go out with me again though."

"She will," John David assured me. "I told her why you did it. 'Course she was freaking out for a while, but she will. Anyway, I meant to have it ready earlier, but I got you another birthday present to make up for you missing the concert. It's in my truck."

We walked to his truck and I saw my bike with a new paint job. He must've snuck it out of my garage at some point. I climbed on and rode around the driveway in circles until my leg felt stiff. I got ready to take a fall, but I hadn't seen that John David caught my bike before I splattered on the ground.

"Thanks John David," I said.

"Anytime," John David said. "Hetero."

The Return

*P*ine Ridge is a big rez, about the size of Rhode Island and Delaware put together, but big as it is, things get around fast. You can't fart without 50 other people knowing by dinnertime on the same day. When a rumor spread that Ignacio was coming back to Pine Ridge, I was the only one who believed it. John David swore it was bunk. The very day Ignacio came back, we rode our bikes around the rez talking about the rumor.

"He's in California, why would he come back to this dump?"

"Maybe he misses you," I said but John David told me to shut up. When he left, we were fresh out of high school. By now, we were down to our last days of college. He was one class away from his Business Management degree and I was a semester away from my English degree. It didn't make sense for Ignacio to come back to Pine Ridge. California was his home. But then again, a lot of things that happen in Lakota territory don't make sense. Wounded Knee didn't make sense. Mount Rushmore didn't make sense. Ina marrying Ate definitely didn't make sense to Unci or anyone else. Anything Ray Firebird said or did never made any sense. Ignacio coming back to Pine Ridge would just be one more thing to add to "No Sense" list.

"If he comes back," John David said as we rode. "I'll punch him in the face."

"What if he said he was sorry for leaving?" I asked.

"Doesn't matter, I'm still kicking his ass," John David said and knowing him, he probably would. We stopped by the Puente house, looking for clues. All the lights were out and Mr. Puente's car wasn't in the driveway.

"Maybe they're picking him up from the airport," I shrugged. "I thought I saw Mr. Puente heading towards Rapid City earlier."

"I thought I saw Mr. Puente earlier too, but it was just a pile of dog shit," John David answered and I almost fell off my bike from laughing.

I was pumping gas in my car at Big Bat's after an emergency night shift at work when I thought I saw Ignacio in front of me. He looked more muscular, his hair was shorter, and his thin mustache was gone. The scar near his right eye gave him away.

"Nimo!" he said. "I got home about an hour ago and I wanted to keep it low-key and then I run into you!" Ignacio hugged me so tight, he lifted me off the ground.

"What are you doing back here? You didn't like San Francisco?"

"No, it was great," he said. "I got my degree in Kinesiology like I always wanted. It's a nice city, gay friendly, but it was missing something."

"Indians?" I asked which made him smile.

"Has JD been with anyone else since I left?" Ignacio asked.

"I don't think so," I said, shaking my head. "He would have told me about it."

"He probably thinks I left him for someone else, but I didn't," he said. "I still love him, Nimo. I didn't date anyone else at school because I wanted to patch things up with him. I hope he doesn't hate me." Knowing the way John David was, I doubted he hated Ignacio. He always said he did, but sometimes I'd catch him staring at his mini Costa Rican flag in his truck. Ignacio gave him the flag for their first Valentine's Day together.

"When do you think I should talk to him again?" he asked.

"Uh, I'd give it a couple of days," I said. "Last week, he said if saw you here, he'd punch you in the face."

"I deserve that," he sighed. He hugged me again and said he'd be in touch.

The next morning, I replaced some light bulbs in the student lounge at Spotted Elk College. John David was there, studying for his summer class. It was a business theory class and it was his second time taking it. If he passed, he'd finally graduate and get to open a restaurant just like the one his ate had in New York City.

"Need help?" he asked from his table.

"No, I got it," I said from my ladder, though I did need help. My leg was acting up again.

"Hey, John David, can I ask you something?" I said as I screwed a new light bulb in. John David nodded. I asked him what he would do if Ignacio really came back to Pine Ridge and wanted to get back together with him.

"I'd shove his sorry ass up George Washington's nose at Mount Rushmore."

"That sounds terrible," I said and stepped down from my ladder.

"What the hell did you expect? Run into his open arms and kiss his face off?"

"Yeah, you see-" I said, but John David cut me off.

"Nimo, I loved Ignacio for a long time, but I've moved on. I don't bother you about Cindy, why do you care about me and Ignacio?"

"John David, he came back," I said before he could keep on yelling. He stood up from his chair, walked over to the window, and pressed his cheek against the hot glass.

"That burned like hell, I guess I must be awake," he said. "Are you messing with me, Nimo? 'Cause if you are, I'll kill you."

"I saw him last night at Big Bat's, he just got here. He wants to talk to you about what happened and how sorry he is, I think you should give him a chance," I said.

"No fucking way!" he shouted. He threw his textbook across the lounge.

"Sorry Nimo, I'm not mad at you," he wheezed. "I'm, ah, I can't even talk." He picked up his textbook and walked out, covering his face with his hand.

A little before my shift was over, Ate and me took all the trash to the dumpster. I told him about Ignacio being back and he already knew.

"But he only got here last night, how did you find out so fast?" I said.

"This is Pine Ridge, son, people knew Ina was pregnant with you before I did," he said. "Is JD gonna take him back?"

"Doesn't seem like it," I said.

"Ignacio could've found a way to keep in touch if he really loved JD," Ate said as he tossed the last trash bag into the dumpster. "When you love someone, you're willing to do whatever it takes to be with them." He took off his rubber wedding ring and replaced it with his golden wedding ring, rubbing his fingers on the surface.

After I clocked out from work the next Tuesday, I drove straight to the Temple of God's Love. They were getting ready to have a service about the Book of Corinthians. Ignacio was at the front desk, greeting everyone who walked in. I squeezed in through the crowd and asked him if he and John David talked yet. He shook his head.

"He hates me, Nimo," he said. "What's the use? Hey, if you wanna stay for the service, we're having dinner after."

Since there would be food, I did go to the service. For the most part, Mr. Puente preached decently until the end when he brought up gay people. I tuned out most of what he said, but I did hear him say gay people have an agenda to convert straight people into being gay. If that was the case, John David and Ignacio weren't doing a very good job at converting me or anyone else.

"Did you like the service?" Ignacio asked as we ate grilled chicken and corn.

"Eh, it was okay," I said. "Your dad gets kinda boring after an hour."

"Yeah, I know," Ignacio said with a laugh. "I've heard that sermon about five hundred times and he still hasn't changed it. It's one of my favorites though."

"Why? Your dad talked smack about gay people again," I reminded him.

"He always does, Nimo," Ignacio sighed. "I don't even pay attention to that anymore. Anyway, the first book of

Corinthians has a couple verses about love in chapter 13. I read those verses in San Francisco whenever I missed JD, which was every day."

While dessert was passed around, I asked Ignacio why he vanished. He said his parents told him if he kept being with John David, they would disown him forever.

"I guess it's tough for you to understand, Nimo. Your parents really love you. I'm sure if you were gay, your mom and dad would love you just the same."

"Maybe you should be having this conversation with John David instead of me," I said. Ignacio stared at the floor for a moment.

"I left him without telling him why," Ignacio said. "I broke his heart into pieces."

"Dammit, Nimo, I told you I'm not talking to him," John David said when I brought up Ignacio during a game of pool at his house.

"I really think you should talk to him."

"Would you be quiet? You're messing up my shot," John David said and then he struck the eight ball into a pocket.

"Loser!" I said and he asked for a rematch. I let him have the first shot of the next game. The eight ball spun right into a pocket on the left side of the pool table.

"This is pissing me off, let's go get something to eat at Big Bat's," John David said. We got into his truck and I noticed his mini Costa Rican flag was missing. I asked him about it and he said he didn't have to hang it up anymore since everyone on Pine Ridge knew he was half Costa Rican.

"Everyone knew you were half Costa Rican when Ignacio gave it to you and you still hung it up," I reminded him.

"Look, it's my truck, I'll do what I want," he said and turned up the radio, too loud for me to keep talking.

"Nimo, JD, my favorite customers," Mr. Graywolf said when we got to Big Bat's. "Your parents came by about an hour ago, Nimo. They bought a mega pack of condoms and ten tubes of lube."

"Gross," I groaned. No matter how many times he told me that joke, it was always gross.

"Your boyfriend's back," Mr. Graywolf said to John David. "He was here yesterday and he also bought a mega pack of condoms and ten tubes of lube."

"Good, he's gonna need that to do himself," John David answered. Claudia eyed me from behind the counter. I said hello and she didn't answer. Ever since I beat up Scott, she wouldn't speak to me. I wanted to tell her, "You need ten tubes of lube to get your big stuck up stick out of your butt," but I kept quiet.

While John David and me waited for our usual hot dog combos, I asked if he really hated Ignacio because I wasn't sure.

"Is the sky blue?" he answered. "Can we just drop it, please? It's over between me and him, Nimo. I don't want him back."

When our hot dog combos arrived, Ignacio walked inside. He stopped at our table and John David went outside right away.

"He doesn't want his hot dog?" Ignacio asked.

"I'll get to-go boxes, you go talk to him," I said. I stepped outside a few minutes later, not seeing John David. Ignacio stood by John David's truck, whistling.

"Where did he go?" I asked.

"He said he had to pee," Ignacio answered. I told Ignacio to sit tight while I went to get John David. I found him sitting by the water fountains next to the restrooms.

"You are not making me go out there," John David said. I made a deal with him – if he and Ignacio didn't make up, he could punch me. If they did, I'd punch him. With that, John David agreed to talk to Ignacio for a couple minutes.

"Honey," Ignacio said to him when we were outside again.

"Don't honey me. What do you want?"

"I want you."

"How do I know you're not gonna leave me again?" John David said. "Prove it." Ignacio reached into his pocket for his wallet. He took out a picture of himself and John David together in our senior year. On the back, he had written "Love never fails. 1 Corinthians 13:8."

"I kept this picture with me the whole time," Ignacio said. "When I missed you, I'd look at it and I would read Corinthians to remind myself what love was because there were times when I'd forget. You showed me what love was."

"I did not," John David said. "Did I?"

"JD, you are the perfect description of what love is according to Corinthians," Ignacio said and touched John David's hand. "But if you wanna find someone else, that's okay. I still love you, JD."

"Just," John David said with his eyes focused on the ground. "Give me a few days to think about this."

After Ignacio left, I climbed into John David's truck and he took me home without saying a word until we got to my driveway.

"What do you think I should do?" he asked. "Would you get back with Cindy if you had the chance?"

"I'd jump off Mount Rushmore," I said. "She didn't love me

the way Ignacio loves you. I loved her but truth be told, all we really did was have sex a lot and make tons of copies at her ate's shop."

"Do you think he's being serious about getting back together?" he said. "I mean, what if we get back together and he leaves me again?"

"Then I'll beat the crap outta him," I said.

"Nimo, Ignacio could take down the Hulk, c'mon."

"I don't care, I already beat the crap out of three guys for you, I can beat up one," I said. John David laughed. He unlocked the truck's doors and I slid out. I watched him reverse and take off at high speed.

The Temple of God's Love has an annual pow wow to raise money for the church's missionary work. I showed up early before everyone else took all the free food. Ate and Ina arrived a little later. Ina was going to be selling her famous jewelry. Ate was going to be at the drum circle, even though his throat was bothering him.

"How are you gonna sing loud enough if you can't talk?" I asked him.

"There's an ancient Lakota secret to loud singing, Nimo," Ate said with strains in his voice. "Think about Ray Firebird completely naked and in your bed next to you."

"You need your head examined, Jay Eagle," Ina said to Ate. They shared a kiss on the lips and went to opposite ends of the pow wow.

Eventually, I found Ignacio at the drink booth serving lemonade to a long line of sweaty people. He gave me a large cup of lemonade with extra ice.

"No John David?" I asked.

"Nope," Ignacio said as he served himself a cup of water. "I don't blame him." He sat down on a cooler and wiped sweat from his forehead with his hands.

"Need a towel?" we heard John David ask. Ignacio looked up at him and he smiled. John David smiled back.

"I need a towel," I said.

"Not you, Nimo, you're not sweating," John David said.

"I could use one," Ignacio said.

"Sorry, I actually don't have any towels," John David said. "Uh, I'm still in love with you, Ignacio, and you know I'm serious 'cause I hate almost everyone. It's a miracle I even like you. There, now put me in front of firing squad and let's pretend this corny moment never happened." Ignacio got up from the cooler and asked him to say it again.

"I love you," John David said. "And I wanna be with you, but I swear to the Creator, if you leave me again, I'm gonna kick your ass from here to the moon, bring you back to earth, and do it a second time. Right, Nimo?"

"Yeah," I said to Ignacio. "We'll send you so far into space, NASA won't be able to find you no matter how hard they try."

"Don't worry, JD," Ignacio said and stroked John David's cheek. "I'm not going anywhere. Hey, Nimo, can you give out the lemonade for a few minutes?" I nodded and quickly got behind the stand. I watched them head towards the parking lot, talking to each other. When they were away from the crowd, I saw them hold hands for the first time in over four years.

The Wedding

J ohn David wanted to go to Jimmy's over in Sioux Plains, his favorite restaurant, for his 24th birthday. While we waited for a table, John David hugged Ignacio and gave him a kiss, despite the stares he got from the other customers. The waitress came and said our table was ready. She led us all the way to the very back, far away from everyone else.

"Happy Birthday, honey," Ignacio told John David, which made him blush. He kissed John David's cheek. John David sunk a little in his seat.

After dinner, we planned to see a movie at the Showtime Center. Ignacio drove slower than usual and took a wrong turn twice. Then Ignacio pulled over to a gas station to use the bathroom for a good fifteen minutes.

"That idiot knows where Showtime is, why the hell are we going on a tour of Sioux Plains?" John David said as we waited for Ignacio in the truck.

"Why aren't you driving? This is your truck."

"Because," he said. "Because, I have no idea. Where are my keys? I'm going to Showtime myself."

"Ignacio took them when he went to the bathroom," I said. John David groaned deeply. He banged his head against the window.

John David sat in the driver's seat when Ignacio came back. Ignacio offered to drive, but John David told him he wanted to see a movie before the world ended. We went down East 11th Street and made a left onto Little Bighorn Drive, right in front of Showtime Center. We walked to the box office to buy our tickets and John David suddenly collapsed on the ground.

"Well?" Ignacio said to him. "Yes or no?" I looked up at the theater's marquee sign. It said: JOHN DAVID GUTIERREZ, WILL YOU MARRY ME?

"You idiot, why were you stalling me?" John David shouted as he stood up.

"I had to, the theater said they wouldn't have the sign ready until 8," Ignacio said. I'd say about 300 people stared at the marquee sign in total confusion with me. Ignacio got down on one knee and proposed to John David. Half of the crowd cheered and the other half pretended it wasn't happening by looking away from them.

"Yes," John David sniffled as he hugged Ignacio. "Hell yes."

"Geez Nimo, we're only gonna be gone for five days," John David said as he put my suitcase into his truck. "What did you put in here? An anvil?"

"No, just a ton of books and some journals" I said and slid into the passenger seat. "Oh, and a big pack of black pens."

"You mean you're gonna write stories in New York?"

"Why not?"

"I don't know how you do it, Nimo. I can barely write my own name and you can write entire stories in a day."

John David and Ignacio picked New York City for their wedding because it was legal and Mr. Gutierrez, John David's dad, lived there. They were engaged for a year and saved every penny for their big day. My parents would leave for New York City three days later with Miss Running Bear. Ignacio's parents were still undecided.

"You think the Puentes will show up?" I asked John David as we pulled up to the Rapid City Regional Airport.

"When those people die, I'm gonna do somersaults the whole day," he said.

"Those people are about to be your in-laws though."

"Yeah, yeah, more like in-flaws," he grumbled. We checked our luggage in and went to find Ignacio at our terminal.

"What took you guys so long?" Ignacio asked us when we found him. "I've been here for an hour."

"Nimo packed a barbell in his suitcase and I threw my back out trying to put it in the truck," John David said. He sat down next to Ignacio and gave him a kiss on his cheek. An old man walking by gave them a sneer, but they didn't notice.

"I'm so glad you and your parents are coming, Nimo," Ignacio said to me. "The wedding would be empty without you and your family."

"It'd be empty without us," John David said. "We're the ones getting married."

While we were on the plane, Ignacio and John David took naps. I was sleepy myself, but I stayed up to write. There was a writing program in Rapid City I wanted to try to get into. The deadline wasn't for another two months, but I felt like I had to write the best story ever. I'm not sure how long I wrote. Eventually I fell asleep and when I woke up, I saw smeared ink all over my hand.

We landed in New York City at eight in the morning. Mr. Gutierrez waited for us in his old Buick. He wasn't muscular like John David, but massively overweight to the point where his belly nearly pressed against the steering wheel. His gray hair was totally flat on his head, like he squeezed an entire bottle of gel into it. He had a small beard filled with a mixture of black and gray hairs. For being in his late 50's, I could definitely see John David's face in his.

"Something wrong, Dad?" John David said as Mr. Gutierrez drove us to his brownstone house in Bensonhurst, Brooklyn through light rain. "You haven't been talking much and you usually talk enough for me to call you Talk-enstein."

"The news said we might be getting a real bad hurricane this week," Mr. Gutierrez said. "I closed down the restaurant just in case it happens."

"In New York?" John David said. "The chances of the Red Sox taking over the Yankees is more possible than a big hurricane." Mr. Gutierrez shook his head.

"No, this hurricane looks like it's gonna be a big one," he said.

I took a nap as soon as I got to Mr. Gutierrez's house. When I woke up, John David and Ignacio asked if I wanted to head over to Coney Island later and I said sure. It was my first time visiting New York City. I wanted to have a decent experience.

"What do you think of my childhood home, Nimo?" John David asked me.

"It's not bad," I said. "Are you thinking about moving back here?"

"What? No way!" he said. "I love Pine Ridge. Brooklyn is huge, but it's also lonely. Nobody knows you here, but on the rez, you know almost everyone. Moving to Pine Ridge was probably the best thing that happened to me after my parents divorced."

"If your parents hadn't split up and my parents weren't missionaries, we would've never met," Ignacio said and rubbed his cheek against John David's nose.

Our plan for Coney Island was cut since the rain grew heavier. We stayed inside instead. I read The Lone Ranger and Tonto Fistfight in Heaven by Sherman Alexie, one of the books I brought with me. Ina called after I finished the first story.

"Is everything okay, hoksila? The news says a hurricane's gonna hit New York."

"It's fine, just raining a lot," I said. "It doesn't look too bad."

"Flights might be canceled if it gets worse. Oh, I knew me and Ate should've gone with you. Do you have enough clean underwear?"

"For the Creator's sake, no child of ours would leave home without 20 pairs of underwear," I heard Ate say in the background. "If Nellie was with us now, she'd be over there with enough underwear to last a year. What about you, Josie? You have so many panties in your dresser, they'll last until your afterlife."

"Jay Eagle!" Ina said. "Nimo, I'm sorry, your ate's being loud again."

"Nellie would be packing underwear in her socks if it all didn't fit in her suitcase! You know it's true, Josie!"

"I'll call you later, hoksila," Ina said. "Be good." I hung up and got back to reading for a few minutes until Mr. Gutierrez called my name from the living room.

"The hurricane is gonna hit after all," he said, pointing to the newscast on the television. "It should come by tomorrow."

"My parents think me and John David caused the hurricane because we're getting married," Ignacio said. All of us laughed loud and hard.

"You tell them I take that as a compliment," John David said. "Our love is so strong, we caused a natural disaster."

Since I was born and raised on landlocked Pine Ridge, I didn't know how bad a hurricane could be. When the power went out and the trees outside the house fell down and the streets looked like canals, I reached my arms up and said, "Creator, go easy on me. I've been a good hoksila, right? I wanna meet Nellie, but tonight!"

"Contain yourself, Nimo," John David said. "The hurricane won't get you."

"How do you know?" I said.

"Because according to Mr. Puente, hurricanes don't come for heterosexuals," he said. Another tree toppled to the ground, barely missing the roof of the house. I fell backwards and hit the floor.

"You need to chill out, Nimo."

"We're all gonna die, John David," I said. "The hurricane's gonna come in here and drown us, isn't it?"

"Would you get up and go talk to Ignacio or something? You're driving me crazy with your optimism."

Ignacio played with flashlights in the guest bedroom. I used to play with flashlights as a kid, but that was because my parents hadn't paid the light bill, not because of a giant hurricane.

"Maybe this is a sign," Ignacio said as the thunder growled. "Maybe it's not right for us to get married."

"What are you talking about?"

"With all this rain and flooding, we can't get married. Maybe we should cancel the whole thing and go back to Pine Ridge."

"Do you love John David?" I asked.

"Of course I do," he said. "There's no one else I wanna spend my life with."

"Then marry him," I said. "I spent 400 bucks on a plane ticket to get here and now I'm in the middle of a damn hurricane! If you don't marry him, I will!" Ignacio laughed and dropped his flashlight on the floor.

In New York, I learned that the biggest downside about a hurricane is the flooding. All the streets were rivers and there was no way to use the subways. But the worst part about the hurricane in this case was the wedding venue. John David used to play at the Great Lawn in Central Park when he was a little kid. Ignacio booked the same area of the Great Lawn John David played in, but the whole place was in shambles after the hurricane passed. It was more like the Great Swamp.

"What is the damn problem?" John David said when we got back to his ate's house after visiting Central Park. We shivered because the heater was dead. "I'm just trying to get married and the Creator is destroying the world."

"It'll be fine soon," I said, but I wasn't even sure. The wedding was postponed and my parents and Miss Running Bear were still in Pine Ridge until travel conditions were a hundred percent safe.

"Nimo's right, sweetie," Ignacio said and hugged John David. "Hurricanes happen every year. We'll be married before you know it."

"Okay," John David sighed. "I waited years to see you again, I guess I can wait a couple more days to call you my husband."

Mr. Gutierrez couldn't stand not working. His restaurant, Tico's, was down the street from his house. Despite Tico's being closed indefinitely, he was still going to provide the catering at the wedding, even though he was having trouble accepting it. Mr. Gutierrez has two sons from his first marriage. They're John David's half-brothers Alexander and Orlando. I never met them and John David told me I wasn't missing out. He only mentioned them to once or twice because he said he didn't even feel like they were his siblings. They refused to attend the wedding. They said it wasn't "real." Mr. Gutierrez freaked out when John David came out. He thought he failed as a father to him.

"Gay?" I remember him saying to John David on the phone. "Is it because of the divorce? Did I not spend enough time with you? I'm sorry for screwing up. I didn't mean you any harm, kid."

"How's the restaurant doing, Dad?" John David asked during our fancy dinner of cold sandwiches for the fifth day in a row.

"No power," Mr. Gutierrez said. "No hot water. Spoiled food. But, no matter what happens, you're gonna get plates of casado at your wedding." Casado is Spanish for married. In Costa Rica, it's a dish with rice, beans, a fried egg, a fried plantain, some salad, and a person's choice of meat, way better tasting than a cold sandwich.

"You mean it?" John David asked.

"Oh yeah," Mr. Gutierrez said. "When I met your mom, she had never eaten Costa Rican food before. I made her a plate of casado on our first date and then again on our wedding night."

"We really appreciate it, Mr. Gutierrez," Ignacio said.

"Are you ever gonna get married again, Dad?" John David asked. "Mom is dating someone right now, not seriously, but you never know. They've only been on two dates so far."

"Me? Oh, no, I've been single since the divorce, I don't think I could get married again. I remember the day I met your mom. It was January 30th, 1983. She was a student at NYU and she was doing a cultural project on Costa Rican cuisine for some class. She walked into the restaurant and my dad said, "Hello, what can I get for you today?" I thought it was love at first sight, but it wasn't. We shouldn't have gotten married so fast."

"Don't regret it, Mr. Gutierrez," Ignacio said. "If life had worked out differently, I wouldn't have John David by my side right now." Mr. Gutierrez looked up at Ignacio and tightened his lips.

"You love my boy, don't you?" he asked Ignacio. Ignacio nodded. He put an arm around John David and kissed his cheek.

"Good," Mr. Gutierrez said. "Please take care of him." He and Ignacio shook hands. Like John David, he wasn't one to talk about or show his feelings. I didn't know Mr. Gutierrez very well. I only knew what John David told me about him. Mr. Gutierrez's eyes swelled up. He was happy or devastated. I couldn't tell.

When it was finally safe in New York, damage was everywhere. The Great Lawn changed to the Great Swamp from Hell. Ina and Ate arrived with Miss Running Bear to Mr. Gutierrez's house on November 8th. The wedding was set for November 10th, 'Normal Day or Armageddon,' according to John David.

"Are your parents coming?" I asked Ignacio the night before the wedding. We sat on the porch, people watching.

"They haven't answered my calls," he said. "Getting married

is a pain in the ass. It's expensive and it sucks all the energy out of you, especially when your parents keep giving you crap. I just want to put the ring on JD's finger and be done with this."

"They'll get over it," I said. "They can't ditch you forever."

"Nimo, when they found out about me and JD, they were furious," Ignacio said. "My dad called me disgusting, freak, and unnatural. My mom wasn't so bad. She told me it was only a demonic spirit and she could pray for it to go away. But I love JD. Nothing this strong can be unnatural."

"You're right," I said. "Don't think about what they said or did to you, think about how happy you're gonna be with John David."

In the morning, my parents and me struggled to get our clothes right. No matter how many times I fixed my ponytail, I still looked like a bum. Ate styled my ponytail in the same way he does his, but it turned out crooked.

"The hell with it, we ain't even going to a straight wedding," he said. "Here, I'll make mine crooked too." He undid his ponytail and sloppily put it back together.

"Jay Eagle, you still haven't put on your good shoes," Ina said from the bathroom.

"This wedding's part Lakota, Josie, I'm going in my moccasins," he said. His 'moccasins' are actually knock off Nike slippers.

"Nimo, you look so handsome," Ina said when she saw me. She pinched my cheeks and adjusted my tie. "I can't wait to go to your wedding someday."

"Ina," I whined. "I told you I'm never getting married."

"Oh Nimo, nobody actually wants to get married. I'm only married to your ate because of his good life insurance policy.

One day you'll find a girl who also has a good life insurance policy and you'll marry her."

"Who is this pretty lady here?" Ate said to Ina when he spotted her in her red dress. "Lady, I must be dead because you look like an angel."

"That's what they all say," Ina said with a giggle. Ate gave Ina a long kiss on her forehead and I caught her blushing. They celebrated their 27th wedding anniversary the previous June.

The Great Lawn was a wreck. Trees were on the ground, leaves were piled up, and benches were crushed. The minister stood at Turtle Pond, under the altar by the brown water. I sat down with my parents on a tangled bench. They left some space between us for Nellie to sit. Mr. Gutierrez and Miss Running Bear were in lawn chairs. Snow started falling, but it wasn't too heavy, luckily.

"This place looks like absolute crap," John David said as he walked to the altar with Ignacio, hand in hand. "Why do I have to get married at a dump?"

"It's not so bad," Ignacio said. "It looks better now that you're here."

"It's freezing out here," John David groaned. "I'm only wearing this rented tuxedo and it's thinner than Ray Firebird's wallet."

The minister started the ceremony off by introducing Ignacio and John David to me, my parents, and John David's parents, as if we didn't know them already. People in the park walking by eavesdropped. Some looked uneasy, some were smiling. I saw a pretty lady about my age. Her face lit up when she saw the wedding ceremony. Her black hair flowed past her shoulders, her body curved around her waist, and there was a big zit in the middle of her forehead. She was so beautiful.

"Ignacio Antonio Puente and John David Gutierrez met each other at Red Cloud High School," the minister went on. "They fell in love with one anoth-"

"They already know who we are," John David said and pointed in the minister's face. "It's freezing out here, that tree over there is about to fall over, and this pond stinks. Marry us now or you'll be sitting in the pond."

"Certainly," the minister nodded. "You and Ignacio may exchange your vows."

Since he was freezing to death, John David said the fastest wedding vows I've ever heard. I missed what he said, but I was sure they were good because Ignacio looked satisfied. My cellphone rang right when Ignacio started his vows.

"Sorry guys," I said and walked away to another part of the park. It was Mr. Puente.

"Nimo! You tell Ignacio I don't care what the state of New York says, he's not married. If he wanted to get married, he should have found a nice girl and married her. Tell him, Nimo! Tell him to stop being a Sodomite!" I was about to hang up, but I heard Mrs. Puente's voice in the background. She came on the phone and told me to listen carefully.

"Tell Ignacio we love him," she said. "Tell him I said congratulations and I'll be praying for a loving, healthy, and long marriage. Will you do that for me, Nimo?"

"I will," I said. "I promise." I hung up and went back to my seat.

"Keep going," I said to Ignacio. "Your mom says congrats and she'll be praying for a loving, healthy, and long marriage."

"What did my dad say?" he asked.

"That doesn't matter," I answered.

"Thanks Nimo," he said. "Anyway, JD, I never told you this

but I knew I was leaving for California and I didn't want to tell you. I figured you'd take it better if you didn't know. But during the time you didn't hear from me, I thought about you every day. And even now, whenever you're not around, I think about you. My parents, well, mostly my dad, tried to rip us apart many, many times, but I want to be with you for good. I love you, John David."

"I love you too, Ignacio," John David said and hugged him.

"Jay Eagle," Ina sniffled and wiped her tears on Ate's shoulder.

"For the Creator's sake, Josie, what the hell are you crying for? Weddings give you bad memories?" Ate said. They turned to their sides to hug each other. I looked to my side and saw the pretty lady was still there, peering over. Ignacio got the rings out for them to say their I do's. They kissed at last and were officially husband and husband.

"Nimo!" John David called to me. "We're married! We finally did it!"

"Huh?" I said, getting back to reality. As I got up from my seat, I made eye contact with the pretty lady, who was now a little closer to us. She stared at me closely and she said, "It was so beautiful."

"It was," I said. "Like you."

The Bullet

I didn't get into the writing program I applied for in Rapid City, but I did get into the writing program at New York University, which is what I wanted anyway. My girlfriend, Oneida Horn, lived in Queens with her parents and her little brother, Daniel. Her ina is Seneca and German and her ate is Mohawk. She's the pretty girl who watched John David and Ignacio's wedding. I didn't want to have a long-distance girlfriend again, but she changed my mind. She and I would be moving into our own apartment in a couple months, right before we started grad school at NYU.

To celebrate my acceptance to NYU, John David and Ignacio took me out to Sioux Plains for dinner, but we spent way too much time bowling, playing pool, and singing karaoke. I wobbled into my house, half-asleep, at past three in the morning. As I turned around to close the door behind me, two men shoved me against the wall.

"Here," I said and handed them my wallet. The joke was on them. After being out all night, my wallet only had eight $1 bills in it.

"No credit cards?" one of the burglars asked. He wore a ski mask and the other wore a nylon sock over his face. I shook my head. They threw me on the floor and ransacked the living room. We didn't have a stash of money, jewelry, or expensive clothes. The most they could take was Ina's knock off china dinner set and my $8.

"All right, kid, where's the good stuff?" Sock Face asked.

"That's it, really," I shrugged. Sock Face punched me in my stomach and Ski Mask kicked my bad leg. They took off and burst through my parents' bedroom. I heard Ina screaming and Ate cursing. I ran over and I saw Sock Face holding Ate against the wall while Ski Mask spread himself over Ina.

"Nimo, call the cops," Ate told me in Lakota. There aren't too many people on the rez who speak fluent Lakota. Fortunately, they didn't. I called 911 and rushed back to the bedroom. Ski Mask tied Ina's hands together and he was trying to rip off her nightgown. I kicked Sock Face in the groin and Ate knocked him down. Then Ate grabbed his handmade spear hanging over the dresser.

"That's my wife, you son of a bitch!" Ate shouted and jammed the spear through Ski Mask's leg as far as he could. I didn't see Sock Face fire the gun. I only saw Ate bleed all over the carpet.

Ate was taken to the IHS Hospital. He lost a lot of blood, but he was stable. The bullet missed his heart by a couple of centimeters. The good news was Sock Face and Ski Mask were found at Big Bat's right after leaving our house. They smashed the glass doors open with hammers. The cops found them thanks to the alarm going off. They were arrested, but that didn't change what happened to Ate. Ina was a wreck. She cried and screamed every time I got near her.

"But Ina, he's still alive," I said and she fell on the floor, sobbing into her hands.

"What if he don't make it?" she cried. "What if they killed him? What am I gonna do without him? I've been with him since I was 19 years old."

I didn't get any sleep the whole night and neither did Ina. Ate was in the trauma center and they don't allow visitors. I sat in the waiting room wondering if he was alive or not. Finally, a nurse told me Ate would be transferred by helicopter to the Sioux Plains Medical Center, where Leksi Gray Mountain and Tunwinla Rosa still worked after all these years.

"C'mon Ina, let's try to get some sleep," I said. "Ate will be okay soon." She hooked onto my arm and walked to the parking lot with me. Ina and Ate have the habit of rubbing their wedding rings whenever they're apart from each other. Even while half-asleep, Ina massaged her wedding ring.

I placed Ina on the couch when we got home. After I plopped down on my bed to try to get some sleep, John David called to see how I was doing.

"I gotta go to Sioux Plains Med Center, they're transferring my ate over there."

"I'll drive you," he said. "Ignacio got the day off and he's making you and your ina some food. Get some shut eye. I'll pick you up in three hours."

Of course, I didn't sleep at all. Every time I tried to, I heard Ate's voice say, "you son of a bitch." He said that a lot when he was pissed off, even to women. If those were his last words, they'd be perfect for him. I went to my parents' room and used Ate's switchblade to cut out his bloodstains from the carpet. The stains were thicker, wider, and caked. I shoved the cut carpet pieces into a plastic bag and stuck them in the garage in case the cops needed them later for evidence. The bedroom actually looked better with giant holes in the carpet.

"Nimo, open the damn door!" I heard from outside. I saw John David standing on the porch with Ignacio, hand in hand. They had been married for six months by now and recently got their own house a couple blocks away from mine.

"Sorry, I didn't hear the doorbell," I said and let them in.

"What doorbell? Your ate never fixed the last one you had," John David reminded me. I went to the couch and tried to wake Ina up, but she didn't budge. With Ignacio's help, I carried her to John David's truck outside.

"Someone's gotta be real sick to hurt your family, Nimo," Ignacio said as we headed to Highway 18. "I've been praying for your dad all morning."

"He must've put up one hell of a fight, huh? Remember how he beat the crap outta that guy in Rapid City for calling your ina a dirty Indian?" John David said to me.

"Of course I remember," I said and cleared my throat for my Ate imitation. "I'm gonna scalp you and hang your hair up in my living room, you son of a bitch." John David laughed and continued with, "Then I'm gonna cut your face off and wipe my ass with it, you son of a bitch!"

"Your dad is something, Nimo," Ignacio said. "You're gonna miss him when you move to New York City."

"I miss him already," I said. I really did.

I found Leksi Gray Mountain at the Intensive Care Unit, drawing on his notepad. He sketches the human body right before a surgery to help him visualize it.

"Everything okay?" I asked him and he dropped his notepad on the floor.

"Oh, hoksila," he said. "You scared me. Your ate was shot four times, but he's okay, nothing I can't fix. The operation will have him back to normal. He got his blood transfusion and his vital signs are doing well."

"He was shot four times?" I said. "They told me once at IHS."

"That's because certain people at IHS don't know how to count to four," Leksi said and showed me his drawing. There were circles on the chest, legs, and arm.

"If you need someone talk to, your tunwinla Rosa is at home today," he said. "Lucy is always up to talk to you, too. She adores you, Nimo. You're like her tiblo."

"I don't want to tell them about my problems, Leksi."

"Why not? Listening to problems is what your tunwinla does for a living. She won't mind. As for Lucy, she spends hours on the phone anyway. She won't mind a phone call from you." He patted me on my back and went through doors which said STAFF ONLY.

Back in the waiting room, Ina finally woke up and was slowly eating Ignacio's famous broccoli cheese casserole. John David and Ignacio looked out the window, hugging each other and sharing kisses in between.

"Nimo, did you find your leksi?" Ina asked. I said I did and we had to wait until the surgery was over. I asked if she was doing okay and she nodded. Part of me wished Ate could be in the ICU for a different reason. If he had a heart attack or an accident at work, it would be expected. Even a car wreck would have made more sense. Being shot was too out there.

When Ate was awake at last, he asked Ina what time it was. She didn't answer him since she wept loudly at the sound of his voice.

"Geez Josie, am I that late for work?" he said. Ina hugged him through the tubes crisscrossing over his body, but he was upset he still didn't know what time it was.

"It's Tuesday and it's 9:16 in the morning," I said.

"Thank you son," Ate answered. "Hey Josie, I told Gray Mountain to save the bullets for me. I'm gonna make a necklace outta them."

"Don't you do that! I don't wanna see those, they almost killed you."

"Aw c'mon, can I keep one? Just one? I'll wear it under my shirt."

"No, I don't ever wanna see those things again," Ina told him. Ate and Ina went back and forth about the bullets for twenty minutes or so. In the end, they agreed on keeping only one. I stayed with Ate in the room while Ina went to the cafeteria to get us breakfast. Ate said he didn't remember being shot four times. The first bullet knocked him out. He told me the pain was very sharp, but it was over quickly.

"Real pain is childbirth," Ate said. "When Ina gave birth to you, she screamed so loud, I lost my hearing for a whole day. She was in labor with you for twelve hours. On top of that, you got my melon head and you almost split her open."

"Ate, stop, I don't need to know," I said, but he kept on talking. He told me every detail of my birth, from the moment Ina went into labor to her contractions and the second my "big, giant melon head flew out."

"You've seen the movie Alien, right?" Ate said. "It was kinda like that, only much bloodier and you weren't from outer space."

"Ate, quit it, that's so nasty," I said with gags.

"Damn straight," Ate said and put his hand on my left

209

shoulder. "I remember the second the doctor held you up, you gave out a big yawn instead of a cry. You were covered in blood and some other fluids. It was the most disgusting thing I ever saw. But that day was one of the best days of my life. I can't believe you're gonna leave the house soon. What am I gonna do without you?"

"I'll be home on holidays. Or you can come visit me. I'm not gonna disappear, Ate. After I finish the program, I can buy a house for you and Ina in New York or maybe I'll move back here." He sat up in his bed.

"Hoksila, you're some kid," he said. "You make our ancestors proud. Mount Rushmore might be the reason people come to South Dakota, but a couple years from today, they'll come because of your stories."

For the first time in a long time, I worked with only Mr. Black Bear at Spotted Elk College. He didn't know as much as Ate and it was hard to work with him since I didn't know as much either. We needed to replace some breakers in the electrical system and we got shocked at least ten times.

"Your ate is an expert with this thing," Mr. Black Bear said. "I'm still learning and I've been doing this work for years now. Your ate is a natural when it comes to fixing stuff. The night before he got shot, he got mad at me for accidentally breaking a pipe in the third floor bathroom. I turned the wrench too far."

"I've done that too, Mr. Black Bear," I said. "It's not a big deal."

"It was to your ate," he said. "He saw what I did and he looked down at me and said, 'Good Lord, Noe, you're about as useless as Columbus Day!'" Mr. Black Bear laughed heartily. For being

Scott's ate, he was much nicer.

"When do you think he'll be back?" he asked. "I miss him. He's a great guy, Nimo. You're lucky to have him for a father."

"I'm not sure," I admitted. "I hope he'll be back soon."

"I'll miss you when you leave," he said. "Scott will too. He might not say it, but he will, Nimo. He's always been jealous of you. I know he's my son, but he's got issues. The only honor he ever got from school was perfect attendance. Mrs. Black Bear always tells him what you're up to. She's so proud of you. We all are, hoksila. There ain't a person on Pine Ridge who don't know how smart you are."

Even with Mr. Black Bear's help, I wasn't able to finish what I had to do in time and I was 30 minutes late to class. My professors knew what happened to Ate, like everyone on the rez did. They said they missed seeing him fixing pipes, waxing the floors, and washing the windows. I told my professors Ate would be back soon, once he was his strong self again, whenever that would be.

"Nimo, did you check if the pipes were working fine?" Ate asked when I got home. He sat in his chair, wearing his bullet necklace, with his new cane next to him.

"No leaks," I said.

"Don't forget to replace the bulbs in the student lounge; they was looking low on juice last time I was there," he said.

"Changed them today," I answered him.

"How was Mr. Black Bear? Did he put water in the electrical system?"

"Some trouble with a couple of breakers," I said. "No biggie."

"Breakers?" he said and held a hand on his forehead. "Oh, geez. He probably electrocuted himself. His brain is as solid as Mount Rushmore."

Ina called out from the kitchen, saying dinner was ready. Ate pressed his hand on his cane and slowly stood up. One of the bullets got a nerve in his right leg, but the cane was temporary. At least I wanted it to be.

"Help me out, Nimo. This pain's a son of a bitch," he said. I reached my hand out and he grabbed on. We're the same height, almost the same weight too. For some reason, Ate seemed much smaller.

"Thank you son," Ate said when he sat at the table. "Hey Josie, this food smells great. This is what Noe Black Bear smells like after getting roasted by breakers."

"It's just something I tossed together," Ina said. "Just a little bit of black beans, rice, and some chicken." She bent over to kiss Ate on his lips.

"Nimo, Oneida called while you were in class. She said your move in date is August 2nd and the apartment has a great view of Central Park."

"I really like her, hoksila," Ate said. "She's sweet, smart, and much nicer to you than Cindy ever was. Are you gonna marry her?"

"Ate!" I said. "We've only been together for six months."

"Young people these days," he said. "Ina and me dated for a year before I proposed. A year after, we were married and here we are now. I knew I had to have Ina when I met her. She's the only woman in the world who gave me warmth in my heart instead of my pants. Put on a ring on her!"

"Jay Eagle!" Ina said. "He'll get married when he's ready. Don't you like her, Nimo? She might be your wife someday."

"Yeah, I like her," I said. "I like her a lot. But c'mon, it's way too early to think about getting married."

Leksi Gray Mountain came over a little after dinner. His

eyes were half open as he checked to see how Ate was doing. He took Ate's temperature, checked his heartbeat, listened to his lungs, and looked to see how his surgical scar was healing.

"I am fine, get on home to Rosa and Lucy, you look like a zombie," Ate told him. "I'm strong, I'll be back at work before you know it."

"Eight to twelve weeks," Leksi Gray Mountain said to Ate firmly. "Not any sooner, misun. Everything is looking good for now."

"Of course everything's looking good, I'm the better looking brother," Ate said. Leksi Gray Mountain was too tired to laugh. He swung his white coat off and carried it in his arm as he walked outside to his truck. I never liked seeing him in his white coat. It always meant someone wasn't doing well.

Ignacio was a personal trainer for the rez gym. He suggested I take Ate to the gym three times a week for strength exercises. When I did, Ate couldn't do anything, not even throw a weighted ball or a push up.

"This is bunk, I lift heavy stuff at work all the time," Ate said.

"But Ate, you haven't worked in over a month," I reminded him. He swore he was still as strong as before and he tried to lift a 100 pound barbell to prove it.

"Baby steps, Mr. Thunderclap," Ignacio said when he saw Ate wasn't succeeding.

"Just relax for now, Ate, you still got plenty of time off from work," I said. He didn't listen. He tried a 50 pound barbell next and he collapsed on the floor.

"All right, let's go home," Ate groaned. I helped him up and thanked Ignacio for his time. Ate was always stronger than me and Mr. Black Bear. He could lift the heaviest equipment without grunting, which wasn't really good because of his heart condition. There were times at work when I'd see him carrying at least 150 pounds worth of machinery and I'd secretly pray to the Creator to keep his heart from popping in half.

"That barbell was a son of a bitch," Ate said during our drive home. "I gotta get back to work before Noe tears the college apart."

"Like Ignacio said, Ate, baby steps," I said. "You're already in six weeks of recovery, you're halfway already."

"Nimo, your ina's birthday is coming up soon, how am I supposed to take her out anywhere if I can't do a damn thing?"

"Take her to Showtime Center, maybe there's a movie she wants to see," I suggested. "She loves movies. Or just stay home with her."

"Nah, your ina likes doing stuff," he shook his head. "She loves going dancing, but I can't dance, not with a cane. I look like I'm 50 years old."

"Ate, you're 51," I said and he hung his head low.

"That's right, son," Ate went on. "I was gonna let those sons of bitches take whatever they wanted, but when one of them tried to hurt your ina, that was it for me. If they killed me, I wouldn't have given a damn. There ain't too many people I'd take a bullet for." We came to a red light I didn't see and I slammed my foot on the brake pedal, making us both lurch forward.

"And you know what? When me and Ina first got married, three guys was bugging her at work. I said I was gonna hang them with their own intestines. Sometimes I hate being her husband. She's beautiful, Nimo, and with her being so beautiful, it means I gotta contemplate homicide at least once a week," Ate said. He didn't stop talking about Ina for the rest of the drive. During the whole time, he rubbed his wedding ring.

John David was the assistant manager at Supreme Harmony, an upscale Chinese restaurant in Sioux Plains. He arranged a cheap dinner for Ina's birthday. Since it was Friday night and my parents would be gone for a long time, I planned a hangout day with John David and Ignacio. We ordered pizza and watched TV in my living room.

"Honey, could you get me a glass of water?" Ignacio said to John David.

"No, get it yourself," John David said, but he went into the kitchen anyway.

"Do you think your dad's ever gonna come to another training session?" Ignacio asked me. I shrugged my shoulders.

"He wants to go back to work next week, but I don't think he's ready. Today, it took him fifteen minutes to open a jelly jar. I'll ask him again though." John David returned with Ignacio's water. He bent over and gave Ignacio a long kiss on his cheek.

"Sorry for the PDA," John David said to me. "It's Ignacio's fault for being so damn adorable."

Skimming TV channels got old after a while. John David suggested we go to George's Restaurant in Sioux Plains. After 9pm on Friday and Saturday, the restaurant transforms into a music venue. We ordered a couple drinks and waited for the atmosphere to liven up. The DJ in the corner of the room put on David Bowie's song "Let's Dance." Almost everyone in the room rushed to the dance floor.

"Dance with me, JD," Ignacio said through the music. He pulled John David from our table and dragged him out to the dance floor. I sat in my chair, watching them take over the scene. They were always great dancers, but people usually stared at them for being a same sex couple, not for their smooth moves. I couldn't dance as well as I used to.

"You tired, Nimo?" Ignacio asked me after he and John David shared about six songs together. "We can head home if you want."

"I'll try to bust a move soon," I said, but I never did. I watched Ignacio and John David dance for a few more songs and then I told them I was heading home for the night.

"Drive safe, Nimo," Ignacio said. "Let's do this again before you leave."

"We will," I said and waved to him and John David. As I drove back to Pine Ridge, I realized I hadn't written anything new since getting into the NYU program. It was actually getting tougher for me to write. I felt like I had already written enough about Pine Ridge and there wasn't anything else to say at this point. I approached my neighborhood in the darkness. Ray Firebird was on the side of the road, wearing a big glow stick around his neck. He leapt in front of my car when I passed him.

"Glad to hear your ate's doing well," he said with the smell of smoke on his breath. "Word around here is you're moving away."

"You heard right," I told him. "I'm moving to New York City in August. I'm gonna get my master's degree over there. But I'll visit Pine Ridge whenever I can."

"You better," he said. "Put me in a story, okay?"

"You're already in a couple of them," I said and handed him a dollar.

"Oh, and I hear you got a girlfriend now too. Do your best to keep her. It's hard to find true love. Mine is beer. Beer never yells at you, not like my old lady used to."

"You were married?" I asked him. "To who?"

"Long time ago, before you was born. Her name was Linda Pinkwater. She ran off with my cousin, Paul Firebird. Last I heard, they had three girls and a boy. She wasn't there for me, kid. Find yourself a lady who's always there for you."

It was past 1am when I got home. Ate's truck was parked behind Ina's car. I figured they were asleep so I opened the door quietly and tiptoed to the kitchen for a late night snack, but then I heard Ina talk over a slow song on the radio.

"C'mon Jay Eagle, it's my birthday," she said.

"Josie, I told you I ain't dancing with you in this condition and that's that."

"But there ain't nothing wrong with you," Ina said. I peeked inside the kitchen, seeing Ina try to lift Ate up from a chair at the table. He wouldn't budge, but after she kissed on his cheek, he wobbled to his feet.

"Aw Josie, I can't do it," Ate groaned as Ina swayed him. "I'm too weak."

"Jay Eagle, don't be ridiculous," Ina said and turned up the radio. Ate barely moved at first. He was able to build up to a faster pace after a minute or two, but then he ran out of breath.

"See, I told you I couldn't, now do you believe me?" Ate said and eased himself back into the chair. "I'll dance with you when I get better."

"But you did dance, even if it was only for a little while," Ina said as she shut the radio off. She sat down next to him, put his cane aside, and hugged him.

"Happy Birthday, Josie," Ate sighed. "Wish I could've given you a good day. Sorry for not being a hundred percent." Ate's bullet necklace came loose and fell on the floor. Ina picked it up and placed it on the table.

"Sweetie," Ina said. "You've given me tons of good days."

"Today wasn't a good day."

"It was a perfect day, I got to spend it with you."

"I feel dizzy," Ate groaned. "I think I'm gonna fall off this chair."

"No you ain't," Ina said and took him tighter in her arms. "I got you, babe."

"Babe, I got you babe," Ate said in his off-key singing voice. "I got you babe."

"Jay Eagle, don't sing, you sound like a hurt walrus," Ina said and he laughed. He looked at Ina, giving her his wink of approval.

"Aw, what the hell," Ate said and stood up without his cane. He kept one hand on the table and twirled Ina with the other.

When I was about to fall asleep, Oneida called my cellphone. She worked as a night shift receptionist for Bellevue Hospital in Manhattan. Every night she'd call to tell me she got to work safely. This time, she called to say something else.

"Nimo," Oneida said in her soft voice. "I think I love you."

"Me? What did I do?"

"I don't know. You're just, you're you. I like the stories you write, I like how nice you are, I like how you supported John David and Ignacio's wedding, and I like that you're willing to come be with me. What's there not to like?"

"Sometimes, after I eat chili, I get gassy."

"Nimo!" she said, laughing. "Chili does the same thing to me."

"Really? When I get over there, let's eat a bunch of chili and compare our gas noises. We'll make a game out of it." I listened to her laugh even louder. I imagined her eyes and nose scrunching up. Great Tunkasila James Eagle was right all along. Warmth in your heart is how you know you're in love.

"Oneida," I said. "Can I tell you a story?"

"You always can," she said. "But a quick one, my shift starts in five minutes."

"Okay," I started. "There was once a Lakota boy who lived on Pine Ridge, behind Mount Rushmore. He had a notebook. He always kept a few blank pages in there, saved to write about a special girl. After a really long time, he finally wrote in those pages."

"What'd he write?" she asked.

"The Lakota boy was really shy and he didn't think he'd ever find a special girl. But he did. Actually, she found him at Central Park. They dated, long distance, for a few months and then, the Lakota boy realized something. Late one night, just before she clocked in to work, he told her he was in love with her, because he was."

The Flight

"I can't believe the day's here," Ate said as he drove me to the Rapid City Regional Airport. "I remember driving you home from the hospital when you was three days old. Today, I'm letting you go. It's the day we always dreamed of, right Josie? As of today, August 1st, we're officially empty nesters!"

"Shut your mouth, you big bonehead!" Ina said. She clutched a wad of tissues in her hand and rubbed her eyes with it. That morning, Ina woke up at three in the morning to make me batches of her dino cookies to take to New York. She couldn't stop crying though. She had been barely able to eat breakfast.

"Geez Josie, I was just joking," Ate said and patted her hand. "I'm gonna miss Nimo too, but he's a big hoksila now. You know the saying – birds gotta leave the nest, especially if they're Ray Firebirds."

"I'll visit, Ina," I told her. "I already got that maintenance job at the hospital where Oneida works, I'll save up and come home for Christmas break, I promise." She grabbed my right thumb and she squeezed it tight.

"Do you have enough underwear?"

"Plenty."

"Don't forget to zip up your jacket when it gets cold," she said. "And turn off the oven after you're done cooking."

"And wipe your ass extra hard after you take a big dump," Ate said. Ina pulled on his ponytail. Soon enough, Ate pulled up to the airport parking lot. He helped me with my luggage and we boarded a shuttle to my terminal. Ina wasn't crying anymore, but she was quiet. I offered her one of the dino cookies she made for me.

"No, hoksila, that's yours," she said, shaking her head. "Don't share them with anyone on the plane either."

"Or Oneida," Ate said. "In fact, don't share anything with anyone. That's the secret to a happy relationship. I never share anything with your ina."

"Oh, Jay Eagle, you were more than happy to share your genes with me when we made Nimo and Nellie," Ina said. I gagged loudly. They laughed and kissed each other.

"The other secret to a happy relationship is to never fight about money," Ate went on. "Your ina and I are still madly in love because we have never, ever fought about money 'cause we don't got no money to fight over in the first place."

"That's true, Nimo," Ina said. "Stay broke with Oneida."

When the shuttle stopped at my terminal, Ate unloaded my luggage again and set everything down on a cart. Ina hugged me with tears all over her face.

"If you don't like it over there, you can always come home," she said, sniffling. "Call me whenever you want. Don't forget to turn off the light when you leave a room."

"Stop it, Josie, you're gonna drive the poor kid crazy," Ate told her. Ina gave me one last hug. I lowered myself down to her height and she kissed my forehead.

"I'm so proud of the man you've become, Geronimo," she

said, tearing up even more. "Keep making me proud, my little hoksila. I know all our ancestors are proud of you right now. I'm going to miss you every single day. I love you so much. I can't believe out of all the inas in the world, the Creator chose me to be your ina. Drink plenty of water and eat your vegetables."

"Josie, that's enough," Ate said and rubbed his hand through her hair. "I'm gonna walk Nimo inside, I wanna talk to him alone. I'll be right back, okay? Please don't cry enough to make a new river, we already got enough of those." Ina sat down on a bench, drying her eyes with another crumpled tissue wad. Ate wheeled the cart through the automatic doors. He picked up my heaviest bag and then placed it back down.

"All back to normal now," he said. "Four bullets couldn't take me down."

"Hope Mr. Black Bear doesn't drive you too crazy at work."

"That man is so stupid, he thinks Sitting Bull was a lazy cow," Ate said. He put his hands on my shoulders.

"You know what I thought the first time I saw you? I thought, 'what? This can't be Sequoia Red Cloud's takoja, he's too cute.'"

"Ate, c'mon."

"Then I thought 'oh shit, I'm officially an ate now and I'm broker than the Liberty Bell.' I don't know what the hell happened, son, but you turned out so great, I'm starting to think you are from the movie Alien 'cause I don't know how you're mine. I never thought I could raise a kid like you."

"Okay Ate," I said with a laugh. "I gotta get going."

"I'll see you when you come visit," he said and put his arms around me. "If you get any strange phone calls, heckle them."

"I will."

"And if your ina ever calls you crying, it'll only be because

Ray Firebird's pants fell down and she saw something, all right? She'll be okay, Nimo. I'll be with her whenever she feels sad. You know how much I love her and how much I love you." Ate took his arms away from me. He put a hand over his face. He wasn't crying like Ina had been, but his eyes swelled.

"Toksa hoksila," he said and hugged me one more time. "I'll miss you with all the pieces of my soul." He walked out through the automatic doors. Ate and Ina turned around to wave to me. I returned their wave and then moved along to check in my luggage and find the waiting area.

Before my plane took off, I thought about everything in South Dakota I would miss. Pine Ridge was definitely one. I'd miss John David, Ignacio, Ate and Ina, Leksi Gray Mountain and Tunwinla Rosa, Lucy, Big Bat's, and even Ray Firebird jumping in front of me. But the one thing that came to my mind was Mount Rushmore. People who visit South Dakota almost always visit specifically to see Mount Rushmore. If it wasn't for Mount Rushmore, hardly anyone would come to South Dakota. Pine Ridge Reservation got some tourists, but not as many as Mount Rushmore did. It's unfortunate because Pine Ridge is right there behind Mount Rushmore. All a tourist would need to do is drive south from the Black Hills National Forest and Pine Ridge would come up. People have fun seeing Mount Rushmore, but they're missing out on a lot. People love Mount Rushmore when they see it, but I have a feeling people would love Pine Ridge Reservation just as much if they got to know the place.

About the Author

Darlene P. Campos earned her MFA in Creative Writing from the University of Texas at El Paso. When she is not writing, she is probably at work, at the gym, or trying to get a decent amount of sleep. She is from Guayaquil, Ecuador but she currently lives in Houston, Texas with an adorable pet rabbit named Jake.